What Reviewers Are Saying

The Wedding Rescue:
Love in Little Tree, Book One

"a full-bodied romance filled
with a lot of emotional layers"

—Long and Short Reviews

Santa Dear

"an uplifting story that will give you the
holiday spirit
any time of the year"

Stand-In Mom

"a runaway good read"

"rich in emotional detail"

Romantic Times Book Reviews (4 1/2 Stars)
"charming romance"

The Marriage Solution

"a sweet story of love and parenting"

This one is for all the parents.

And as always, for my husband,
the most loving dad ever

Cover design by The Killion Group, Inc.

ISBN: 978-0997894424

COMING HOME

Love in
LITTLE TREE

BOOK FOUR

MEGAN KELLY

CHAPTER ONE

Reining in her gelding, Cooper, at the top of a hill, Carrie Moore surveyed the ranch house before her. Stiff tufts of grass sprouted sparsely throughout the dry Montana land. She suppressed a curse aimed at Ryan Winslow, her brother-in-law. He'd let his family's ranch fall to ruin, rented it out like a hotel to strangers, and squandered the potential and beauty of the property. All to chase a rodeo prize.

An up-sweep of dirt behind the house caught her attention. No one should be there to stir up dust. Only her cattle grazed over here at Windy Glade these days, and the Moore ranch hands had settled them farther out when the latest batch of renters arrived a few weeks before. Ryan's parents had leased grazing rights to her a year before they died, selling off their cattle as too much to handle with Ryan at rodeo. In Carrie's opinion, they'd lost their joy in the land without their son showing an interest in returning.

She touched her rifle scabbard, glad she never left her ranch without protection, though she hoped the dust-kickers actually were a couple of stray cattle from her place. A command to her horse made him pick up his pace. He proceeded with both speed and caution, not making undue noise. Used to approaching skittish cattle, Cooper did the equine equivalent of tiptoeing toward the Winslow house.

Her former ranch-manager-turned-boyfriend, Matt Reynolds, had gone over as a favor to her to "help" the renters move out three days before, and he'd reported no visible damage to the house or outbuildings. The rental company Ryan used to advertise the place paid Moore Ranch to secure the windows and doors and unplug the refrigerator, a job she usually gave to whichever hand volunteered. Everybody could use an extra buck.

Despite trusting Matt's assessment, Carrie needed to check the house herself to salve her conscience. Her sister, Hannah, would have expected nothing less. Carrie had promised Hannah she'd keep an eye on the ranch next door after Ryan's parents had passed on four years before. Even though Hannah had been dead for two years—maybe *because* Hannah had died—Carrie wouldn't go back on her word. She'd been raised better. In a small town like Little Tree, people took care of each other. She also had to safeguard her niece Sam's legacy.

Most of the renters had been useless big-city partiers, but at least this bunch hadn't brought in—or mishandled—any cattle during their stay. "Duding it up," as one group had put it last year, having more money than sense. Who rented cattle for a few weeks' fun, for heaven's sake? She hadn't even known renting cattle was a thing.

Last week's group had ridden their horses too hard and partied as though Windy Glade housed a college fraternity. She hadn't regretted seeing them go and hoped they hadn't returned to the empty house. A hard swallow accompanied her unease. Confronting a bunch of drunken men wasn't her idea of fun. She could, and had, handled rowdy men over the years, of course, managing Moore Ranch after her parents passed away, but she never got used to it. She'd look into the situation and go for help if needed. She had no illusion of being either Wonder

Woman or Wyatt Earp.

Carrie approached the house from the back, riding in a wide arc in case she needed to flee—in which case, she also didn't want to be seen. Cooper, sure-footed and swift, must have sensed her hesitancy, for a shiver of tension ran through him.

Her heart quickened when she spotted the small figure in the distance, and she pulled the horse to a stop, squinting through the August sun for a better look. Could that be Sam?

She chided herself for wishful thinking. Just because the girl stood on Windy Glade property didn't make her Carrie's beloved niece.

But the girl had the Moore coloring. Light brown braids hung beneath a small dark cowboy hat. Dusty brown boots kicked at the dirt. Hands were tucked in the girl's front shorts pockets, underlining her boredom. She appeared to be about five years tall. Carrie's heart thudded and she had to swallow the lump of tears in her throat. She hadn't seen her niece for a year. The girl's dad, her sister's widower, had cut off communication after the funeral. No more pictures or hastily written anecdotes came in Carrie's email, keeping her updated almost daily on

Sam's little milestones. No more weekly long-distance phone calls or video chats to keep their relationship alive.

All that had died with her sister. Except for one brief encounter last year at the diner where she worked part-time, Carrie hadn't seen Sam. She'd lost her sister and her niece, the latter being Ryan's fault. It wasn't right, and Carrie had a hard time thinking anything charitable about Ryan. But she'd try. For Sam's sake.

The pickup truck parked by the house explained the mini dust storm. They must have arrived as she'd topped the rise. Either Ryan had purchased the same model and color truck—then beat it to hell with a baseball bat—or he still drove the same heap of metal he'd owned for ten years. She'd been too enraptured with Sam to notice his vehicle when he'd stopped in at the diner last year, but she recognized it now.

She took a deep breath and prepared to encounter her brother-in-law—or whatever he wanted to be called now with Hannah gone, severing the family tie. He'd been her neighbor all her growing up years, and she forced herself to remember that boy. His lack of communication after the funeral, cutting her off from Sam, could have been grief; not informing her of his new cell phone number or email address was just cruelty. Tamping down her excitement at seeing Sam again, she urged Cooper forward with a squeeze of her knees.

Soaking in the sight of the small girl before her as she rode closer, Carrie scanned the child's appearance. She believed Ryan would take care of Sam, but a single dad didn't have the same priorities a woman had. A lone cowboy cared about his cleanliness right before competition photos and on Saturday night before hitting the town. Carrie frowned at the idea of Ryan with another woman, but she had to be realistic. Hannah was gone, and he was a man. A single man. A single, handsome man, she admitted. Though to her, he'd always just been Ryan, first the neighbor kid, then Hannah's boyfriend-turned-husband.

At this distance, the girl appeared rumpled and slightly dusty, as one would expect after a child's long car ride. Relief swept over Carrie, easing her continual worry. Losing touch with her niece, with her last tie to Hannah, had cut her to the quick.

The wooden screen door opened, and Ryan emerged, his tall form as familiar to her as if she'd just taken his photo. A light blue chambray work shirt covered broad shoulders. Battered jeans encased his long legs. His once-tan cowboy hat covered his light brown hair and shadowed his face, hiding dark brown eyes that used to sparkle with devilment when he looked at Hannah.

Carrie's breath caught; the extra fabric triangle around his neck hung too long to be a bandana. The slant indicated it should cradle his left arm. She frowned. What had the fool cowboy done to himself now? And why wasn't he wearing the sling properly?

Rolling her eyes, she could make a pretty accurate guess. Ryan would regard the sling as a sign of weakness, and not only of his arm strength. *Men.*

She and Cooper trotted into the ranch yard, drawing Ryan's gaze. Sam backed over to the truck and stood at her father's side. Closer now, Carrie could see the resemblance between her niece and her sister, and herself, for that matter, in the girl's brown eyes and small oval face. Sam had grown a foot and looked more like a short, thin adult than a toddler.

She'd changed so much since Carrie had seen her briefly the year before, it broke her heart. Why had Ryan shut them out?

As she closed the distance, Carrie noted Sam's clothes appeared more than merely rumpled. The girl sported a stain on her belly, near an older tear and an empty buttonhole. Her blue denim shorts appeared hard worn. Judging from the uneven frayed hem, they'd once been jeans. She'd probably grown too tall for them and Ryan had "fixed" the problem with a pair of scissors.

While she inspected Sam, she noticed Ryan's lips tighten in what no one would mistake for a smile.

"Hello, Carrie." His voice came out as smooth as spring water on a summer day and about as chilly.

Instead of dismounting without an invitation, she nodded in return. "Ryan. Hey there, Sam."

A tentative smile hovered on the child's face. "Hi."

"You can't expect her to remember you," Ryan cut in. "She's only seen you roughly two or three times in her life."

His accusing tone stung. Well, the gloves were off, it seemed, though all she'd done was say hello.

What the hell was wrong with him? *Of course* they knew each other. She used to laugh with little Sam and Hannah every week via video calls. And if the girl had forgotten her in the past two years, the child would be reassured by Carrie's resemblance to her mom.

Carrie tamped down her ire and kept her voice sweet and reasonable since Sam listened with an avid expression and wide eyes. "Let's think, Ryan, why would that be?" She shot him an extra sunny smile she hoped would fool Sam. "It isn't as though you've given me your current cell phone number. My emails bounce, and I don't have your rodeo itinerary."

And it's tearing me apart. I miss her so much.

He shrugged—with one shoulder, she noted—and glanced down at his daughter. "Sam, this is Mommy's sister, which makes her your Aunt Carrie. We met up for dinner last year." He glared up into Carrie's face but kept his tone even. "Met her at the diner where she works, so it would have been hard for her to say no."

Outrage burned through Carrie at the unwarranted jab. She patted Cooper's neck, steadying the horse who picked up on the tension. Keeping the child in mind, she responded in a gentle tone. "I would never have turned down the chance to see *you*, Samantha. I'm glad your father could make the time to stop as you *passed through* Little Tree."

Ryan grunted and swiveled to the truck bed.

Sam looked up at her with a solemn expression. "I remember you."

Relieved, Carrie almost melted off of Cooper. She smiled at Sam as she swung down.

"Daddy, do we still got the picture of Mommy and Aunt Carrie and me when I was just a baby?"

"It's in your duffel."

Touched, Carrie had to swallow. She determined to take a photo of herself and her brother Adam with Sam during their visit. The remaining Moores. She turned to Ryan with concern. "What happened to your arm?"

"Fall."

His genetic makeup made him economical with words. Although used to taciturn cowpokes, she didn't appreciate having to drag details out of him. "How?"

"Saddle bronc riding." He handed a brown paper

grocery sack down to Sam. Holding it in both arms but not staggering under its weight, the girl headed toward the house. "It's what I do."

Carrie tossed the reins over the front porch rail. Ground tied, Cooper wouldn't run off if she dropped the reins, but she looped the leather over the wood to buy time to form a civil response.

With the girl out of hearing, Carrie asked the question that had burned in her gut when she'd identified the truck. "Are you still chasing the buckle or have you wised up and come home for good?"

Ryan scowled. "Why are you off your horse? Did I ask you to stay?"

"Nope," Carrie countered sunnily, "and you didn't ask me to visit in the first place, yet here I am."

"Here you are," he said hollowly. "Why?"

"Matt, my..." —she'd leave personal details unspoken— "manager said the last renters were hard on the outside of the house. A Moore Ranch hand usually unplugs the fridge and locks up, but I figured I'd inspect the inside. These last people were over-aged frat boys. Your rental manager needs to do better screening."

"Stop harping."

"I'm not. I'm bringing you up-to-date on property you haven't cared to visit in two years. Honestly, Ryan. You didn't even stop at Windy Glade last year during your fly-over."

He turned his back to her while he dragged more bags to the edges of the truck bed. "I care about Windy Glade. I didn't visit then because it was rented out. And it wasn't a fly-over. I stopped at Leo's."

"I didn't know you were coming. It was only a guess I'd be working that day." She huffed out a breath. "If you're going to detour to Little Tree, at least let us know. You didn't come out to our ranch so Sam could see Adam. He was so hurt to have missed her."

"I figured he was probably hung over."

Carrie fought back her immediate urge to defend him. "Adam is trying to stay sober. You'd know that if you were here."

The grunt from Ryan could have been doubt or from physical pain. His determination to do everything himself exasperated her. "Let me help with those bags. Then I'll inspect the property with you."

He straightened and reported stoically, "The

renters left a mess of empty Scotch bottles and beer cans in the kitchen, but there's no structural damage that I could tell."

Translation: *he and Sam would manage fine, so please go home, Carrie.* Although imagining him saying *please* might be a flight of fancy on her part.

"That's good news then." She turned as the screen door squealed open. Sam slid out of the shadows and moved closer to Ryan. She had obviously keyed in to Ryan's gruffness and sensed something amiss to make her edgy.

"Thanks for checking on us," Ryan said. "We'll see you around."

Rude statements like that for instance.

Carrie couldn't believe he'd have the gall to dismiss her. She had no intention of leaving with Sam acting so uneasy with her. She strode over to the truck and grabbed a backpack.

"What are you doing?"

"Helping a neighbor. Helping a family member. Take your pick." If she smiled any harder at him, her teeth would fall out. She slung the pack over her shoulder.

"Family." He said it as though the word was new

to him. The way he acted, it might well be. "Doesn't mean I have to let a girl tote for me."

Carrie picked up two plastic grocery sacks. Although she'd recently turned twenty-seven, she hadn't felt like a girl since taking over the family ranch eight years before. Nor did she back down from irritating cowboys. Matching him glare for glare, she wished for another four inches so she didn't have to tip her head to face him eye to eye. Not that she wanted to be six feet tall, but the extra confidence wouldn't go amiss.

With a sharp pivot, she turned toward the front door. Inside, the smell of sweat and dirt and alcohol hung in the stagnant air. She flung the backpack in the general direction of the sofa, watching it send up a dust poof when it landed before she set the grocery sacks on the worn Formica kitchen counter. The refrigerator chugging away wouldn't be cold enough for food for at least half an hour since Ryan must have just plugged it back in. Unable to recall whether he did much planning, she hoped he had a cooler and ice in the truck.

Just then, the door behind her creaked open and then slammed shut. Ryan had stubbornly looped *four* grocery bags over his right arm. Wait—was he limping? Sam trudged by her, hauling a faded black duffel bag almost as long as she was tall, with a handle looped over each shoulder. A trail of slightly cleaner floor followed behind her where the bag dragged on the ground. Obviously, Ryan hadn't told the rental management company to send the cleaners before his visit, and she wondered if they'd come to clean before the last renters had arrived. She suspected they'd grown lax with an absentee owner. It might have been months since this place had been attended to properly.

She could barely control a sneeze, and the stale beer smell nearly gagged her. The original hardwood floors were gray with dust; clumps of dirt from muddy boots littered the entrance and living room rug, and the stench of barley, hops, and locker room hung in the air. Poor little Sam could probably get drunk on the beer fumes alone. It gave Carrie a headache.

Or maybe that was Ryan.

"Stop." She put her hands on her hips and frowned at Ryan as Sam stumbled to a standstill. "This is ridiculous. You can't stay here."

"My house, my choice."

Carrie gestured to the dust across everything. "Unless you're filming a remake of *The Grapes of Wrath,* this place is going to take major cleaning and airing out before either of you can sleep in this sty."

"I imagine there's a broom."

She set her lips to keep from telling him where she'd like to shove that broom. Instead, she strove to keep her tone calm and reasonable. "I imagine there is. And I imagine this place works fine for you if you're used to pool halls and back alleys, but you can't expect Sam to stay here. Why don't you both come home with me, at least for tonight?"

His mouth tightened against the reply he probably wanted to make, just not in front of his child. "This is our house."

"Yes, I know," she replied with exaggerated patience, "and your choice. I heard you the first time. That doesn't mean you can breathe without choking." She wanted to add that he appeared to be one-handed as well, but no cowboy wanted his vulnerabilities pointed out.

"I appreciate your worries," Ryan said, "but Sam and I can handle this."

The girl scooted to his side, where he dropped his hand to her shoulder. Sam watched her, unblinking. The girl could be thinking anything from *we're a team* to *save me*. They stood as resolute as a brick wall—with Ryan about as deaf to good sense. Carrie's heart ached to see them united against her. She knew when she'd been beaten.

This round, anyway.

Arguing with Ryan would only scare Sam. Carrie headed to the door, not stopping as she threw over her shoulder, "Put the damned milk in a cooler."

Standing on the porch at Windy Glade brought back memories of Hannah, which, after two years, sliced as sharply as if she'd just heard about her sister's rodeo accident. The memory of Ryan's broken voice at the gravesite saying goodbye to his wife always made Carrie tear up.

But that didn't excuse his absence. Chasing the big buckle, the grand prize in the saddle bronc riding event, had become his all-consuming focus. Carrie missed her niece and wondered how she fared with a single-minded, single dad.

And what about those comments about their last drop-in visit? As though Carrie would ever turn down a chance to see Sam. Was he *insane?*

She mounted Cooper and glanced at the sky. "I tried," she told Hannah.

Her heartache carried her through the ride home and half an hour of cleaning out the barn as the sun set. If she happened to imagine taking the shovel to a certain stubborn male head, no one knew but her.

In a way, she was glad he'd acted like a bull, all ornery and tough. She remembered him as her sister's teenage boyfriend and had felt such sorrow for him when Hannah passed. She'd cut him too much slack for keeping Sam away on the road. But he was no longer the boy next door with no siblings. The adult Ryan made Carrie yearn for her camera to capture the allure of a handsome cowboy—right up until he opened his mouth.

But he and Sam were family, so she trudged inside and thawed some stew, then sent the pot and some bread over to Ryan's with a ranch hand. She pushed stew around on her own plate, not having much appetite while her niece ate a meal and laid her head down next door. Acres of heartache lay between the two ranches.

Determined not to think of Ryan for the rest of

the night, she pulled out a photo album from childhood and spent an hour in the past. Pictures of Hannah confirmed Sam's resemblance, although more blond highlights threaded Hannah's brown hair. Carrie traced a finger over her sister's features. She soaked in the memories evoked by a photo she'd taken after one of Hannah's many triumphs barrel racing as a teenager. The shot of Hannah smiling with pride at her baby girl closed Carrie's throat. Tears pricked her eyes, and she brushed them away.

Not so easy to brush away were thoughts of her niece: poor little Sam over in the Dust Bowl. Hannah would have had her hide.

With a sigh, Carrie headed out the door once again.

~~~

Night fell hard and fast in Montana. Ryan's arm ached like a son of a bitch due to over-exertion. They'd been cleaning for an hour before food arrived to sidetrack him. After noticing the dust on the dinnerware, he'd quickly washed some plates, which Sam had dried. He chewed both resentment and gratitude along with the tender beef, but it was still the best stew he'd ever eaten.

Hell's bells. Did Carrie have to be right about everything? Only pigs could live here. The last renters had apparently left every window open to the dusty wind during their two-week stay. When the windows got shut, everything settled and the place was stifling. He tasted dirt with every breath. While he welcomed the rental money, he resented the renters' intrusion. No one else should be in his family's place, dammit.

Carrie's reference to *The Grapes of Wrath* might have been a gross exaggeration to make a point, but Ryan couldn't claim to be proud of the way his home looked. He could almost feel his parents spinning in their graves.

He made his way upstairs with no one to see how he pulled himself up the handrail except Sam, who was used to his occasional struggles after events. They'd mopped and dusted, and he'd flipped the girl's small mattress—with no little grunting and too much cold sweat—then helped her remake the bed with fresh white sheets he'd brought. He'd probably have nightmares himself about the freaking mattress and his efforts to conquer it with his bad shoulder. He'd ridden wild broncs more cooperative.

Ryan glanced at his old room and determined it needed more work than he had in him. Might as well bunk out on the floor near Sam. He wasn't likely to get a good night's sleep without strong pain killers, and he wouldn't take them until he could be sure Sam wouldn't have a nightmare. As that was always a possibility these days, he settled for an anti-inflammatory to take the edge off. The ibuprofen, washed down with whiskey, didn't do a blessed thing for the pain, but once it kicked in, he'd feel less like banging his head against the wall until he passed out. He had a couple of stronger pain pills from the rodeo doc, but he'd yet to take one. He couldn't risk being zoned out when Sam needed him. He tossed his sleeping bag on the now-clean floor of her room.

She watched him from under a top sheet, despite the heat. A plastic toy horse a little bigger than her hand lay on her pillow. She'd taken to calling the horse "Charming," though he couldn't fathom why. The only good thing Ryan could see was it could be dunked in the tub with her every Saturday night.

"Are you going to sleep in my room, Daddy?"

The hope on her face had him swallowing hard with love and guilt. Humbled that she needed him so much, he knew he should do better by her than this hovel. "You bet."

"All night?"

"Sure thing. If you wake up and I'm not sacked out here snoring, it'll be because it's morning, and I'm downstairs making breakfast."

"Okay." Her small voice indicated her unease with the idea of him being elsewhere, despite her agreement.

"Speaking of breakfast, I'm going to double-check that the refrigerator's working." He smiled and stood. "It was wheezing harder than ole Gus did on a winter morning."

Sam had learned to ride on Gus, as had Hannah and her siblings. Ryan had given him to a farmer before coming home, unable to charge him anything due to the horse's need for meds. The farmer had four-year-old twins who were thrilled to have a gentle gelding to learn to ride on. Ryan wished he hadn't mentioned the horse to his daughter, who'd had a tearful goodbye with Gus.

It seemed everyone and everything she loved was gone except Ryan. That had been one good reason to come home to heal at Windy Glade. Carrie and her brother, Adam, lived right next door—a short ride by truck and a reasonable ten minutes on horseback. They were Sam's only family other than him. If he could forget what Carrie had said at Hannah's funeral, if he could face all the memories of their two ranches which haunted him with happy days that would never return, if he was strong enough to stay here to heal up, then maybe his girl could get to know her aunt and uncle. He found it almost unbearable to be home without her, without his parents. But it had been two years of just him and Sam, and his girl deserved more. A stronger safety net. This last fall had knocked some of the stubbornness out of him.

His little girl needed to be a rancher, not a rodeo circuit rider. He'd have to see about getting another gentle mount for Sam, maybe next spring. After the championship, after his winter commitments. Another expense on his ever-expanding To Do list.

A vehicle pulling into the yard had him turning to the window, left open to air out the place. "Hello at the house," a female voice hollered.

Ryan's jaw tightened before he turned to reassure Sam. "Sounds like Aunt Carrie's back."

He pulled the sheets up to Sam's chin. "I'll see what she wants."

Ryan trotted down the stairs, each jolt vibrating through his shoulder like a sledgehammer hitting a metal spike. He tried to be reasonable and not blame his pain on the woman on the porch, but reasonableness and Carrie never mixed. As a teenager, she'd watched him with her sister like a mama grizzly protecting her cub. He'd taken to ignoring her, but he'd always wondered if she reported his misdeeds back to her parents.

Hannah's funeral had been the last straw. He'd wandered around half-dazed, going through the motions. No wife. No parents. Just his little girl to keep him sane. After the crowd left, Carrie suggested she take in three-year-old Sam. Losing Sam would have devastated him. Ryan refused, and they'd parted with hard feelings between them. It had taken almost six months for Ryan to understand Carrie's need to hang on to her sister through Sam. He knew, because he saw Hannah in Sam every day. Maybe Carrie had thought to ease his burden, but Sam had been his only reason for living back then. Carrie's insensitivity still rankled, making it hard for him to be civil.

The door opened and Carrie walked through without knocking. A pretty wise move, since waiting for an invitation would have been futile. Then he noticed what she carried, and all thoughts of turning her away vanished.

"I brought pie."

His mouth watered. Would she have remembered his favorite—*made* his favorite? This girl had developed a woman's wiles for sure, and he admitted to softening a bit despite being able to see through her tactics.

"I hope Sam likes cherry." She set the pie plate on the scarred wooden table. "I snuck it out of the diner when I left work earlier. I'd appreciate you two helping me finish it off."

Not Dutch apple pie then. He couldn't help smiling at his foolishness, as well as the idea that the diner owner, Leo, would ever deny Carrie anything she wanted. More than likely, she'd found the pie plate on the seat of her truck, a present from her cranky admirer. Back when she'd waitressed for Leo in high school, the old man had treated her like a favorite daughter and turned a beady eye on any male who showed interest. Since her parents had passed away, Carrie needed someone to help run off the vermin looking for a fun time. Her older brother, Adam, should be watching out for her, but he was probably friends with all of the good-for-nothings in town.

It occurred to Ryan he hadn't seen her in a year. She probably had a boyfriend. Surely she'd have let him know if she'd gotten married. A frown formed behind his eyes. It might have been from the pain, but he figured the discomfort stemmed from conscience. He was her brother-in-law, after all. Hannah would have kicked his butt for not keeping in contact. She'd always been the one to do that family stuff. Growing up an only child to parents without siblings, he didn't know much about family obligations now that his wife and parents had passed.

Except for those obligations he had to Sam. He owed it to her to make contact with the Moores and try to mend fences. So he'd come to Windy Glade, doing exactly that. He would put the past behind them and move forward, forging a family for Sam. He took a breath.

That new leaf had to be turned now. There wasn't time for resentment over past injuries. "You got a steady fella?"

Her mouth went as wide as her brown eyes. "What?"

"A beau." Ryan forced himself not to squirm. He sounded ninety.

"I know what a steady fella is. I'm just wondering why you're asking."

"We're kin. I'm supposed to know." When she continued to frown, he added, "Hannah would want us to try to be closer."

Carrie's sigh whooshed out. "I'm seeing someone regular."

His gaze flew to hers. Dammit. He should have known this already. "Who? Is it serious? Is he good enough?"

"He's a steady fellow in all ways. I'm dating Matt Reynolds."

"Your *manager*? Why that son of a—"

"My *former* manager," she cut in. She smiled at some private joke because nothing here was funny that Ryan could see. "He went to work at the Olsteen place before he ever asked me out."

Ryan's chest squeezed at the fondness in her tone. Stupid conscience would keep him up with indigestion all night. "You have wedding plans?"

"Nope."

He waited the required eight seconds. "You want to expand on that?"

"Nope."

Ryan didn't see the point in arguing with a woman. She'd do whatever she pleased. He grunted to let her know of his displeasure but let it go. "Thanks for the pie."

She glanced at the stairs.

"Sam's in bed," he added, "but we'll have it for breakfast."

"Breakfast."

Her flat tone substituted for a thousand words of sermonizing over nutrition for growing girls. He hunched his shoulders and immediately regretted it as pain slammed him. His left arm tingled, and he rubbed his hand against his thigh, hoping she'd assign some other meaning to the action. He didn't intend to broadcast his weakness. "Okay, okay. I'll give her some after lunch if there's any left. Want a piece?"

He crossed the kitchen, intending to distract her from his pain with sweets. Lifting his arm to yank open the small knob on the cupboard made him grit his teeth. Grasping a plate or a glass for milk might be impossible with her for an audience, even with his battered right hand. He turned, dampening the hope from his voice. "Unless you have to run?"

"I came to talk you into coming home with me. Sam can't stay here until it's cleaner." She glanced around, then frowned. "You've done a good job already, though. The place smells more like pine cleaner than beer, at least."

"That almost sounded like a compliment. Did it hurt?" Maybe if he insulted her, she'd leave before he crumpled to the floor. He edged away from the cupboard as though he'd forgotten his offer, hoping she'd forget too and leave.

He needed a pain killer. Bad.

~~~

An hour later, he needed more than Vicodin, whiskey or the combination of the two. Sam had attached herself like a leech, although slightly more adorable. Less adorable was her high-pitched screech that hadn't ceased even after he'd stopped up the mouse hole. The poor critter had likely been scared into anemia when it popped out and twitched its whiskers at Sam.

When had she developed this confounding aversion to rodents? Lord knew, plenty enough crept around the barns and under the stands on the rodeo circuit.

She hung on his good arm, if it could be called that, and lifting the bad one was beyond him, so he knocked at Carrie's screen door with his boot. He balanced on his bruised leg rather than trying to kick with it. He wanted a hot shower and a soft bed, preferably both, and preferably back at his own place. And maybe a stiff drink. None of that appeared likely to happen. "Hey, Carrie, Adam, open up. It's Ryan and Sam."

He barely heard her approach, then suddenly she stood backlit by the kitchen light. He wished he'd brought the pie to sweeten her up, although she'd gotten what she'd been nagging for ever since seeing them earlier.

"What are you doing here?" She pushed open the screen door.

Ryan stepped up but was almost dragged back

on the porch by a statue named Sam. "Come on, little buddy. This is where we're bunking tonight." He turned back to Carrie. "That is, if the offer's still open."

"Of course. Come on in. What changed your mind?"

Sam sidled into the house, eyeing the baseboards.

Ryan grinned. "There's a mouse in our house."

Carrie nodded, her gaze on Sam. "It sounds cute when you say it like that, but they can be quite frightening."

"It wasn't a cute mouse," Sam blurted out, her earlier reticence evaporated. "Not like Cinderella's friends. It was dirty and sneaky."

"Now, how could you know it was dirty?" Ryan chided. "It barely stuck its nose out to say howdy before you scared it away."

"Everything in our house is dirty."

He winced. Out of the mouth of babes.

To her credit, Carrie didn't gloat. "I've got plenty of room here and no mice."

"How do you know?" Sam bent at the waist to check under the old white-washed wooden table.

"Until that mouse jumped out at me, we didn't think we had any either."

"Good point," Carrie said, "but we have a cat."

Sam's smile bloomed. "You do? In the house?"

"The cats live in the barn." Carrie pulled out a chair and without hesitation, Sam did likewise. They sat as comfortably as old friends, talking about Blackie, the mouser, who deigned to wander through the house on occasion.

Ryan leaned his hips against the kitchen counter. You wanted this, he reminded himself. Wanted Sam to know her family, wanted his child to have more than him to rely on if things went south. He only wished it didn't hurt so much to see Sam bond with a woman other than Hannah.

"There are milk and cookies if you want a bedtime snack," Carrie said.

Sam smiled. "I only get to eat cookies on Saturdays. At bedtime, Daddy only has whiskey."

"That is so not true, Samantha." Ryan shook his head. "I sometimes have beer."

She nodded, gaze on Carrie, who filled a cup with milk. "But not cookies, even on Saturday."

"Not even then for a grouchy bronc rider," he

acknowledged. "Cookies are for good little girls who do their chores, brush their teeth, and keep their mouths shut."

Sam giggled, easing the tension across his shoulders that had bunched during her earlier bout of terror. She hadn't screamed like that since those nightmares right after Hannah died. The nightmares had returned a few weeks ago after his injury and made her moan or cry out, but nothing like when the chuck wagon rolled over Hannah during the race, breaking her spine. He swallowed hard against the memory, his chest aching with grief. Being at Windy Glade, their home together for such a short time, brought back all sorts of memories for him. Seeing Carrie, who shared traits with Hannah, piled on the heartache.

Carrie watched Sam dunking cookies in milk as though the girl had invented a new activity. Her intensity gnawed at his gut.

"We're pretty beat," Ryan said. "Do you have a room with two beds? If not, a room with space on the floor for me to stretch out would do."

"That's not necessary. I have two empty bedrooms."

Sam jumped up. "Daddy has to sleep by me when we're someplace different, so he doesn't get scared."

"I see."

Ryan sweated it out while she nodded slowly, taking in Sam's big eyes and pale features. She probably thought of him as a bad parent. Hell, she wouldn't be far wrong. He barely had two cents to buy the necessities.

"We do have twin beds in one room," Carrie said, "but I don't know if you'll fit, Ryan. They're not overly-long."

He pictured his feet dangling off the end of a bed too narrow to turn over in. Not a problem: he'd slept in worse. "It'll be better than the floor."

Sam drained her cup then grabbed his "good" right hand and swung it while he blanked the agony from his face. "And you won't have to worry about a mouse running over you like if you slept on the floor."

He ruffled her hair. "There's that silver lining I overlooked."

Sam beamed a smile so endearing, he couldn't be grumpy, no matter his pain. "Let's go get you tucked in then," he said.

"Daddy, I need to wash my feet first."

He noted her hastily pulled on canvas shoes. "How'd your feet get dirty?"

"They touched the floor the mouse ran on."

Carrie laughed. "I'll show you the bathroom. Do you have a bag?"

"I couldn't bring anything from *there*, other than Charming." His little tomboy shuddered. "All our clothes have to be washed. *After* we get rid of the mice. Could we please borrow your cat?"

"If you like. Who's Charming?"

"I am." Ryan kept a straight face, even when Carrie laughed as though she considered that claim ridiculous.

"My horse." Sam pulled the horse from the waistband of her pajamas.

Carrie made appropriate admiring noises, ending with, "I see why you named him that."

Ryan set his jaw. Now the two of them were in on the secret. What appeared so obvious to Carrie and so obscure to him? It was a damned plastic toy.

"Where's Adam?" Ryan asked. Might as well get this family reunion over with. Or started. Whichever.

Carrie glanced down at Sam. "Your dad means my brother, your Uncle Adam. He'll probably be coming in later, so don't be surprised or scared if you hear some noise. He's bigger than a mouse, so it's hard for him to sneak up on anyone."

"Big like Daddy?"

"Yep." Carrie ran her gaze over him, and he straightened reflexively. "Well, a little taller. A little less wiry."

Sam laughed. "Daddy's not made of wires."

Ryan could have disagreed. His insides had twisted like high voltage lines, some sparking hot and some coated with ice, stiff and unmoving. Seeing Sam open up to Carrie made those wires writhe inside him like snakes. He forced himself to be happy about their relationship blooming. He'd come home partly for this reason, other than not having anywhere else to go until he could compete again. Sam *should* get to know Carrie and Adam. Where would she go if something happened to him? He'd simply have to cowboy-up and ignore the occasional pinch of grief.

Once Sam had the water running in the bathroom sink and couldn't overhear, Ryan asked,

"Where's Adam, really?"

Carrie frowned. "I'm afraid he's at Buck's."

"Buck who?" When she didn't answer, he remembered. "Buck's Bar? Aw, hell, Carrie. Is Adam drinking again?"

CHAPTER TWO

Carrie held in a sigh and lifted a shoulder as though Adam's drinking problem didn't warrant discussion. No inconvenience, just a part of her life. "He's mostly been on the wagon. Sometimes he hits a bump."

"That son of a bitch."

She couldn't blame Ryan for being angry, but her instinctive response to defend Adam kicked in. "It's not his fault. He has an illness."

"That doesn't make it easier on you."

"Actually, it does," she said. "If Adam went drinking for fun and then wasn't able to help around here, I'd resent it. If he came home hungover all the time, wasting our money for no reason, I'd be angry. But he can't help himself."

"You two always did stick together."

"Yeah, we did." She didn't want to mention what it had been like for her and Adam to live in their sister's shadow. Their family activities had revolved around Hannah competing in barrel racing from the time she first qualified up until she married Ryan. She had broken records with her natural ability and often been crowned rodeo princess for her beauty. Neither of the siblings had resented her, but it had been easy to get overlooked with a genuine star shining in their midst.

"When did you become so understanding and grown up?" Ryan asked.

Carrie smirked. "I don't know about the understanding part. Even knowing his alcoholism is an illness, I still get crazy-mad sometimes."

"At least you're human. I began to wonder."

She gave a passable attempt at laughter. "I'm all too human. Selfish, angry, bitchy, you name it. I just try to keep the negative traits in check."

Ryan glanced at the bathroom door, behind which Sam attended her bedtime needs again. "I'm familiar with that trick. Doesn't always work."

Sam came out then, dressed in Carrie's pink T-shirt with "Walk for the Cure" spelled out in silver glitter. It fell well past her knees, emphasizing her smallness and making her appear fragile. Carrie spent hours worrying about her niece. Seeing Sam here softened her anxiety.

"Pink is your color," she told the girl.

Sam beamed before fingering the remaining sparkles on the design.

"Do you wear a lot of pink? Today you wore brown and I'm pretty sure last year when we met at the diner you wore tan."

Ryan did a double-take.

Carrie laughed at him. "Remember? I took a picture of you together."

"Pink is hard to keep clean at rodeo," Sam said matter-of-factly.

Ryan frowned. "You can have any color you want, sport."

Carrie hadn't meant to cause a disagreement. "Keep that shirt to sleep in if you like. It won't matter if it gets stained, since only you and your dad will see you use it for a nightgown."

Ryan glared at her before he turned to Sam. "If you want a pink shirt or nightgown of your own, honey," he said in a gentle voice, "I'll get you one.

You don't have to wear hand-me-downs, especially something that doesn't fit."

Sam looked at the floor. "It's okay. I don't need any new clothes."

His smile stretched thin. "You let me know when."

"I will, Daddy."

Carrie stood two feet away and could have been on the moon for all she felt excluded. The bond between Ryan and Sam couldn't be mistaken.

She wanted her niece well taken care of, but, dammit. Did he have to be so perfect? She yearned to spend time with her niece, meaningful time, not merely a dinner or a sleepover. But there didn't seem to be a need for her in Sam's life.

Was he thinking of everything? Sam should be enrolling in school now for the fall. Did he plan to home-school the girl himself as they traveled the rodeo circuit? Had he made plans for that, requested the materials, signed up for registration, or researched how that all worked? Recalling her argument with Ryan after Hannah's funeral, Carrie didn't want to upset him by asking right now. With his unpredictable streak, he might pack up and leave the area tomorrow.

Perhaps she could talk him into letting Sam stay with her again overnight during their stay, maybe followed by a girly shopping trip. It wouldn't make up for the past two birthdays and Christmases she'd missed, but hopefully they would form a bond. Maybe Sam would want to visit with her and Adam for a few weeks each summer.

Already anticipating the visit, Carrie led the way upstairs and ushered them into the guest bedroom. "It hasn't been used since... Well, for years."

Ryan shot her a look, glanced at the two beds and then at her. "This was Hannah's room. And, I'm guessing, your room."

She nodded. "There's the window you used to throw rocks at."

"Daddy!"

He smiled down at his scandalized daughter. "Your mama slept in this room. I never knew she shared it, although she mentioned us not waking up her little sister."

Carrie winced at the description. She'd been three years younger, not a toddler. "Everyone knew you two snuck out in the dead of night."

"Da-add-dy!"

Carrie and Ryan laughed.

"You're ruining my rep," he said. "I thought we'd been pretty quiet."

"Oh, you were," Carrie said. "Other than rocks hitting glass like a summer hailstorm. Or the horse whickering in the middle of the night right up by the house where it shouldn't be. Or your old pickup crunching across the rocks in the drive, slow and sneaky. Or Hannah thunking against the house as she climbed down from up here." Carrie laughed. "*Of course* we woke up. It sounded like we were under siege."

"It kind of takes the romance out of it that you all knew."

"Dad would have shot you if he didn't believe you were serious about Hannah."

Sam gasped.

"Not really shot him," Carrie rushed to reassure her. "I meant your grandpa Hank protected your mom. She was his little girl, no matter her age."

"Your dad trusted us?" Ryan said. "Never could tell it by the way he used to eye me."

Carrie smiled with soft nostalgia. "He couldn't

very well approve of you running around with his teenage daughter until you declared yourself. Just think of how you'll behave when Samantha brings home a boy."

Both her guests stared at her as though she'd been smoking loco weed. "Not going to happen," Ryan said.

Sam shook her head. "I don't like boys except Dad and Gus."

"Gus?"

"My horse."

Carrie would have guessed that dear old oat-bag had passed already, but she refrained from saying so. "Did you know your mom and I and Uncle Adam all learned how to ride on Gus?"

Sam shook her head with a soundless "wow."

"And yeah," Carrie said, "I agree. Horses can be more fun than boys."

"Hey." A shimmer of humor graced Ryan's mouth.

The girl's ponytail bobbed up and down as she agreed. "Boys are mean and dirty. They pull my hair and put spit on my boots."

Ryan stiffened, eyes narrowed. "Who's been

doing that?"

"Roger and Terry and Mike. Little Mike, not Mickey or the older Mike."

"Do people tell you that's a boy's way of showing how much he likes you?" Carrie asked, ready to call BS on the idea. "Because it's not true."

Sam scowled. "That's not liking me."

Carrie laid her hand on the girl's shoulder. "Honey, they're boys. There's no understanding them."

"Hey, now—" Ryan said again with mock outrage.

"Did you spit on Mommy's boots?" Sam asked. "Or just throw rocks at her?"

Carrie couldn't hold in her laughter, even when Ryan mirrored his daughter's scowl.

"I pitched tiny pebbles at your mom's *window* to get her attention. So she'd know I'd come to pick her up to go for a romantic ride in the moonlight. I did not throw rocks at her, spit on her, or pull her hair."

Sam tilted her head. "Why didn't you knock on the door?"

He blinked. Carrie couldn't wait to hear this answer. He couldn't very well admit he'd been sneaking off with Sam's mom to make out. And probably more.

"It was late at night," Ryan said. "I was being considerate."

Carrie bit back a smile at his attempt to sound virtuous.

Sam climbed onto a bed and bounced a few times. "If Mommy and Aunt Carrie both slept here, how did you know who would come to the window?"

Ryan looked at Carrie as though he'd never seen her before. She shrugged to indicate the thought of meeting him for a moonlight rendezvous had never occurred to her either. She barely remembered when he hadn't been Hannah's boyfriend. They were a matched set.

"Your aunt knew I'd come for Mommy."

"I was too young to go out for a moonlight ride," Carrie filled in.

"How old do you—?"

"Thirty-five," Ryan said, "and that's enough talk about you dating."

Sam scrunched her nose. "Don't want to anyway."

"Good." He turned to Carrie. "Thanks for letting

us stay tonight. I'll rout out the mice, uh, mouse at our place, and be out of your hair tomorrow."

"No hurry. It's nice to have family stay over." Carrie bent and kissed Sam's head. The girl froze as though playing Statues.

Carrie straightened. "Sorry. I forget I'm a stranger to you. I've known you since before you were born."

Quicker than light, Sam scrambled to her feet on the mattress and threw her arms around Carrie's neck, hanging in mid-air. Carrie staggered, the girl's weight a sweet burden. She hugged Sam close, feeling her fragile bones through the nightshirt.

"I don't mind you kissing me," Sam said. "Only I never smelled nobody else who smelled like Mommy. All the ladies who hang around Daddy at rodeo smell like perfumes. Or like horses."

"It's the soap." Carrie set her feet on the bed, trying not to think about the ladies hanging around Ryan or how they might treat Sam. "This has been my favorite all my life, and your mom's as well."

Sam sniffed her own arm. "Do I smell like Mommy?"

"I don't keep my soap in the downstairs

bathroom. The good-smelling stuff is in my room." She swallowed hard. "You can use some tomorrow morning. And I'll wrap up a piece for you to take home."

"I can afford to buy her a bar of soap."

Carrie pivoted to him with a sharp retort, but her irritation faded when she spied his tight mouth and pinched eyes. Must be the mention of Hannah hurting him. Or the idea that now he'd be smelling Hannah's scent again. "Ona Hanson doesn't sell it out of her house anymore. The Catch-All—that's the grocery co-op store in Little Tree that sells local goods," she told Sam. "They carry it. Ona called it 'the pink soap' but they call it Country Blush." She cleared her throat, awkward in the silence. "Well. Let me know if you need anything. Goodnight."

Walking down the hall, she heard their voices low, then fading, then gone. It tore at her heart. Soon they'd be gone from her house, too, back to Windy Glade, then leaving the area. How long before Ryan stopped in at The Diner again or brought Sam to Little Tree for another extended stay?

Could she convince him to leave Sam with her for some visits? Maybe while he practiced for rodeo or when the competition standings grew more intense? Sam was half-Moore after all. She should get to know her mom's side of the family and Moore Ranch.

Tomorrow Carrie had to work at the diner during the late shift. She had chores to tend in the morning and had planned to ride out with the hands, though she wouldn't now with Sam here. Every opportunity she could make for hands-on management of Moore Ranch came as a welcome break from the paperwork. Each time she rode across a field, roped a cow, or helped to birth a calf, she felt the pull of generations of Moores tugging her. She saw what they'd seen in the land, in the green grass or brown dirt. Felt it to her bones. She sensed the determined sense of permanence in the building of the first house on the old homestead, then the second house here when roots were set down.

Hoping Adam came home on his own and the sheriff didn't call her to bail him out, she locked up and headed to her room, setting her cell phone to charge on her bedside table. Just in case. With a little thrill, she snuggled in bed thinking of what to make Sam and Ryan for breakfast, a meal Adam never ate with her.

Most of her family surrounded her. Life was good.

~~~

By the next morning, Carrie had revised her outlook. Too much family could choke a gal.

Breakfast had been less blissful than she envisioned. Ryan wore the clothes he'd arrived in the night before. His early morning stubble coupled with the blue work shirt made his dark brown eyes more arresting, a thing she'd never thought before. She bet those "perfumed ladies" flocked around him.

He didn't say a word, only grunted what she presumed were thanks before digging in to ham, eggs, fried potatoes, bacon and toast. Sam, still in the pink T-shirt, went round-eyed over the hotcakes before heaping three small ones on her plate and slathering them with sweet syrup. Before long, she wore a white milk mustache and a maple goatee.

At least Adam hadn't shown his bleary-eyed face yet. Carrie could only be thankful not to deal with Ryan confronting her presumably hungover brother.

After breakfast, Sam stayed by her side as though she were an extra appendage, almost tripping her while Carrie tried to do chores in the house then out in the barn. The girl stumbled against her while keeping an eye out for the cat near the stalls. Ryan loomed behind them, making sure Sam didn't get hurt, hovering and herding them like a giant cattle dog. Even Cooper nudged the feed bag to urge her on with what the horse no doubt considered should be her main concern, feeding him.

"Why doesn't the cat come out to see me, Aunt Carrie?"

"She has new babies. They're shy of people since they live in the barn. Let me finish feeding this mare and I'll show you how to call them out."

"I can do that," Ryan said.

Sam turned wide brown eyes on her father. "You can call the cats?"

"I'm not a cat wrangler, kiddo. I'll feed the stock."

After a moment's debate, Carrie handed him the oat scoop. She'd rather spend time with her niece anyway. If he hurt his shoulder worse, it wouldn't rub on her conscience. Darn cowboy still wouldn't wear the sling. When she'd asked about it at breakfast, he'd leveled a look on her and changed the subject.

"Come sit here." Carrie plopped onto some clean hay lying loose on the floor, and Sam followed suit. "Now, twitch this stick of hay back and forth. That's good."

Sam pushed at the hair in her eyes, leaving a thin streak of dirt. "Do you whistle at them like horses or dogs? I want a dog, but Daddy says no. I can't whistle yet anyway."

Carrie would have given her anything she wanted, but she tempered her response. No use walking into the middle of a dispute. "It would be hard to train and work a dog when your daddy has to practice bronc riding. Ranch dogs don't like to sit idle."

"I have to sit around a lot of times while Daddy rides. The dog could be comp'ny."

Carrie caught sight of a brown kitten with two white paws and bounced the end of her hay stick up and down. The feline went down on its haunches, instinct kicking in. Carrie kept her gaze on Sam as though the kitten went undetected. Mama Blackie must not be far away. "Did your daddy ever tell you about my horse when I was just a little older than you?"

Sam shook her head. "I don't think so. What about it?"

"I couldn't have a dog either. My mom didn't like dogs or cats underfoot in the house, and my dad didn't want to bother with a pet who didn't earn its keep. When your Uncle Adam turned eight, he tried to sneak a dog home, but we had to return it because it belonged to our neighbors."

"To Daddy?"

"Our other neighbors, not as close. Uncle Adam had pretty much had to carry it to our house."

"I thought this was a story about your horse."

Carrie bumped her shoulder against Sam. "Be patient. I was about seven when this part happens. One of our mares gave birth and my dad said I could name the foal whatever I wanted. So I called him Fido."

Sam chuckled at her. "That's a dog's name."

"But I couldn't have a dog. I figured it was the next best thing. My dad grumped about it, but he'd made a promise. So the poor horse went through life called Fido. I never got that dog."

"Where's Fido now?"

"He caught a really bad cold and passed away."

"Like my mommy." Sam tilted her head in question. "But you're all growed up. Why don't you get a dog now? I could play with it for you while we're here."

"A dog's a lot of work."

The girl sighed with her entire body. "That's what Daddy says."

Carrie considered buying her a puppy and dealing with the fallout afterward. Better to ask forgiveness than permission. If Ryan drew a hard line in the dirt, Carrie would take in the dog herself and Sam could come play with it. Win-win.

The brown kitten pounced on Carrie's hay stick at the same time as the black and white mother cat grabbed Sam's stick. Blackie flopped on her back and swatted at the straw Sam dangled above her.

"You can pet her," Carrie told Sam. "Rub her under her chin, but not her tummy where her milk is. She's probably sensitive there."

Sam giggled as the mama purred and captured her hand with its paws.

"Don't let that cat scratch her," Ryan said.

Carrie glanced up, surprised to find him watching from the door of the far stall, which housed a mare due to foal soon. Most of the horses had gone out with the men, who were herding cattle and fixing fence line. The pregnant mare and Cooper had been left behind.

"I won't get scratched," Sam said, pushing at her hair with her free hand.

"Blackie is vaccinated," Carrie assured him. She fished in the pocket of her denim shorts and emerged with a powder blue elastic hair tie, which she held up to Sam. "May I?"

The girl nodded. Carrie raked her fingers through the honeyed brown strands, carefully working out knots. With several quick twists, she French-braided Sam's hair, as best as circumstances allowed, and gathered the end up in the tie.

"There. Princess Samantha."

Sam grinned and touched her hair. "Is it pretty?"

"It would be better if I had a brush, but you look sweet."

"Daddy?"

Ryan glanced over. "What?"

"Is my hair pretty?"

"It's out of your face." He turned away before

either female face formed a scowl, which happened right quick.

"You are *very* pretty," Carrie said.

Sam nodded, her gaze on the kitten, who had abandoned Carrie's straw and lay on its side, half asleep. The two other kittens hadn't made an appearance, too shy to approach.

"Do you want to bring him inside? I'll grab up his mom, Blackie here, and they can make sure we don't have mice."

Sam shrugged and raked her fingers through the hay.

Carrie wanted to smack some sense into Ryan. Sam had barely outgrown her baby shoes, but she already needed male attention and reassurance. Namely, his.

Scooping up the mama cat, Carrie showed Sam how to hold the kitten securely. The brown ball of fur snuggled into the girl, as though to disprove that being a barn cat made him uneasy with people. Sam grinned as the kitten gave a sleepy little purr.

"He doesn't have a name yet," Carrie said as they walked into the house. "If you promise not to call him Fido, you can name him."

Sam laughed. "I wouldn't name a cat Fido."

"You're smarter than me, then." She held the screen door open for Sam. "What do you think would fit him?"

"I don't know." Sam scrunched up her nose as she set the kitten on the kitchen floor. "Since his mom is Blackie, maybe we should call him Brownie."

They watched as Blackie strutted across the room with the kitten gamboling behind.

Carrie pointed. "See how casually they're walking around? If there were mice in the house, Blackie would be on their scent already. I'm sure we're safe."

"Do you like my name idea for the kitten? I'm not sure it's the goodest."

"The best," Carrie corrected. "Brownie's a good name, but it's only the first one you came up with. Why don't you make up a list this afternoon while I'm at work? We can go over it tomorrow or whenever you finish." She patted the girl's bony shoulder. "If after all that thinking, you want to call him Brownie, then you'll know it's the best name for him."

"Okay, I'll make a list, but I don't spell as good as some of the kids. 'Cause I'm only five."

Carrie's radar went on alert. "Do you practice writing with your dad?"

"Sometimes. I'm too little to go to real school, but Daddy said probably next year. I play School with my babysitter sometimes."

"You make what letters you think are right." Carrie couldn't wait to see how much Ryan had been teaching Sam. The girl should at least be forming the letters in her name by now. "You can read it to me because you'll know what it says."

"Okay."

"And don't compare yourself to the older kids. They probably don't take care of their dads as well as you do yours. We all have our strengths."

Sam giggled. "I don't take care of Daddy. He takes care of me."

"I saw you unloading the car and taking stuff upstairs. Most five-year-olds would have left that to the adults, but you were helping."

"Daddy has a bad arm." Sam's eyes went wide. "Don't tell him I said that. He don't like people to know."

"I already knew. I saw his sling."

Sam nodded. "He don't like to wear it, but I told

him 'doctor said to' so he does. Sometimes."

"And you don't think that's taking care of him?"
Carrie shook her head. "I doubt he'd do anything he
didn't want to for anyone *except* you."

Sam beamed. "Really?"

"He's always been stubborn."

"I heard that," Ryan said from the doorway.

Both females screeched in surprise and spun
toward him. Carrie put her hand over her mouth to
hide a guilty smile, even knowing he couldn't refute
her words.

"Daddy, you scared us. Aunt Carrie's going to let
me name this kitty."

His brows lowered as he shifted his gaze between
the two. "As long as you understand it's Aunt
Carrie's. No bringing it home."

"I know," Sam said.

"Understood," Carrie said.

"I finished feeding the horses in the barn. I want
to head over to home and do some more cleaning. We
need to stay in our own house tonight."

"I want to take Blackie," Sam insisted.

"That okay with you?"

Carrie nodded. "She's showing her kitten how to

inspect the house for mice now. They'll be a good team."

"I don't need the kitten."

Sam gasped. "You can't take the kitty away from her mom."

Ryan studied his daughter then sighed. "No, I guess I can't."

To bedevil him, Carrie said, "There are two more kittens in the barn. They should probably learn too."

He shot her the stink-eye but having his daughter in the room hampered his response. "I'll go round them up. You want to give me a hand, sport?"

As they left the house, Carrie put together a bag with cat food and two plastic cereal bowls. She extended it to Ryan when he and Sam returned bearing the cats.

He regarded the bag as though it held rattlers. "What's that?"

"Food and bowls. One's for water."

He opened his mouth.

"Blackie finds her own food in the barn, but she'll eat this stuff. It's a *loan*," Carrie rushed on, feeling a tiny bit contrite over manipulating him into taking all three kittens and Blackie. "I want those cats back. But in the meantime, you can use them to seek out the critters and make sure others don't come in to replace them."

"More would come in?" Sam sounded appalled.

"Not if you have my cats there." Carrie put on a fierce face, glaring at Ryan, and shook a finger at him for good measure. "But you have to return them. Understand? They have work to do in the barn."

He smiled, obviously catching on. She hadn't made him the bad guy, denying his daughter a pet. "Clear as a bell."

"I have to work at The Diner this afternoon, but I can keep Sam here until then." Not that she had any idea how she'd do chores with the girl around. Her desire to have Sam visit long-term collided with reality. But other parents managed farms and kids. She could learn too.

"I want to go with you, Daddy."

"Couldn't manage without you, sport."

That quickly, they closed their family circle, leaving Carrie on the outside.

~~~

Work that night at The Diner kept Carrie's hands and feet busy, but her mind wandered. She tried not to let her worries intrude on her work, but the customers seemed unusually demanding, which meant she didn't pay them the attention they deserved. As the sole waitress on the dinner-to-close shift, she kept moving. And of course, news of the catfish special had spread, a treat to these beef ranchers. Some of them didn't take leisure time for fishing.

Word had, of course, already spread that Ryan had returned, and she spent half her time fielding questions. Not that she had answers. Between taking orders and chatting to locals, she wondered about Sam's life on the rodeo circuit.

To Ryan's credit, the girl looked well-cared-for and seemed happy. Carrie didn't know much about what went on in the mind of a child, however. As she cleared tables toward the end of her shift, she recalled Sam's insistence Ryan sleep in her room so *he* didn't have nightmares. Carrie hadn't been fooled. What nightmares did Sam experience? The girl had been three years old when her mother had died in a horrible accident. Did she remember anything from that time, or was it just the loss, the hole Hannah left that frightened her? Or, worse, had Sam experienced things in her daily life since then that let the bogeyman into her dreams?

Every time the thought rose, Carrie tried to shake it off. Ryan loved Sam, and Carrie trusted him to take care of Sam. But who cared for the little girl when he trained and competed? What did Sam do during the day? Carrie didn't know anything about their life; it seemed as though when they left Little Tree, they were swept into a black hole. And the thought of Sam disappearing again for who knew how long worried Carrie more than anything.

A person stepped in front of her, and she snapped to attention, blinking as though coming out of a trance.

A smile lit her insides when she recognized the man in her path. "Matt. I didn't know you were coming in tonight."

Her former foreman grinned in return and slid into a chair. "Thought I'd surprise you."

Matt Reynolds had moved on to manage the Olsteen ranch two months prior, then had promptly asked Carrie out for a date. He epitomized the cowboy in her mind: strong, rugged, and quiet; more comfortable on a horse than anywhere else. Luckily for Carrie, he was also funny, well-educated, and cared deeply about the same things she did. It didn't hurt he was six feet of muscle with brown eyes she got lost in and was a pretty amazing kisser. The black of his hair spoke to either Native or Spanish ancestry. He'd never investigated his heritage, nor did he intend to. Because he and his younger brother had been abandoned, Matt claimed he didn't care about any family other than the one who'd adopted both boys.

When he'd appeared on her porch, hat in hand, and a blaze of awareness in his expression, she'd been flattered. He'd never shown any inappropriate interest when he'd worked for her. But when he admitted he'd partly taken the other job so he could honorably date her, her knees had gone weak. They still tended to do that when the two of them were alone.

Matt glanced around the room. "Busy night?"

She nodded. Three tables held customers, all finishing up. "Has been."

Good lord, she'd started to talk like a cowboy herself. Two-word sentences, low syllable count. "Word got out we had a fresh fish delivery."

"I heard. I'll have that if there's any left."

"Should be." Carrie took his drink order and sped off to compose herself. Jeez. Had she become so entrenched in ranch work she couldn't make conversation?

She put in his order with Leo in the kitchen and filled a glass with water for Matt.

"Thanks," he said as she set it on his table.

"Long day?"

"Same old, same old. I came late to see you. Hoped you wouldn't be busy."

Carrie checked but didn't see anyone needing her. And this being Little Tree, they'd simply holler for the check or a refill—or get it themselves. Leo's diner defined "casual." Sliding into a chair across from him, she folded her hands on the table to contain herself, beaming with excitement. "Ask me what's new."

Instead, Matt took a long, slow drink of his water, eyeing her over the rim. She couldn't help but grin at him for teasing her. Finally, he said, "Okay, I'll bite. What's new?"

"Sam and Ryan are home."

Matt's brows rose. "That is news. Haven't heard

it from anyone else. How long they been here?"

"Since last night. They tried to stay at Windy Glade. I'd ridden over for a check on the property, and to get out for a ride with Cooper after a day of paperwork. Otherwise, I might not have known they'd come home either."

"Did I miss something wrong at their ranch? Those last renters destroy anything?"

Carrie frowned. "I don't think so."

"You said Ryan and Sam tried to stay there, implying they didn't."

"Oh that. Yes, yes, something was *very* wrong at the ranch. There must've been three inches of dust on every surface. I couldn't let them stay there."

His brow rose. "Three inches?"

"More or less," she conceded.

The bell dinged, and Carrie rose to collect Matt's order from Leo. Her boss stopped her. "I cooked up the last piece of catfish while I was at it. You or Matt can take it home."

"Thanks, Leo. I'll tell him."

"I can't use one serving," he muttered, trying to cover his kind heart with gruffness. "Can't have food go to waste neither."

Having worked for Leo since high school, she saw right through him. He knew Matt lived alone and had to feed himself when he didn't eat at the Olsteen bunkhouse. Being with the men all day then eating together could build bonds, but sometimes the foreman needed a break from the men, and vice versa.

Carrie set down his food, cleared dishes from another table and refilled drinks for two women deep into conversation. While she tallied the bills for the other table, she chatted while the customers paid. She liked her fellow townsfolk, but she wanted to talk to Matt about Sam.

Once the other customers cleared out, Matt paid so she could close out the cash register. Then she sat with him while he finished his dinner, since the scent of cleaning products ruined a meal. Leo clanged around cleaning the kitchen, giving them a semblance of privacy.

"So," Matt said, "I can see something's going on. Sam looks healthy?"

Carrie nodded.

He tilted his head in question. "Happy, well-adjusted?"

"I suppose so."

Matt set down his fork with a laugh. "You sound disgruntled. Did I spoil the news with my summary?"

"No, it's not that. It's... I don't know. I want her to be all those things. Healthy, happy, well-adjusted. I don't know how she could be, though, given her lifestyle. Maybe I'm missing something."

"Why would she be otherwise?" When Carrie didn't answer, he filled in, "Because Hannah's dead? Because Ryan's a man alone, trying to raise a child?"

"No, of course not. Or at least not *just* that. Single dads can raise kids as well as single moms can."

"But?"

"But they live on the rodeo circuit."

"Ah." Matt picked up his fork and scraped the last of the food from his plate.

"She doesn't have a permanent home. They travel all the time and live out of a truck or cheap motel rooms. What about her schooling? She has none."

"Isn't she like, four?"

"She's five."

"Well, I don't want to argue with you, sweetheart,

but what schooling do you expect her to have had?"

"You can't walk into kindergarten knowing nothing these days. Even when we went to school, we already knew colors and letters and...whatever."

"Okay. I don't remember that exactly, but let's say it's true. Are you saying Sam doesn't know colors or letters or" —he grinned— "whatever?"

She resisted being charmed by him, barely. "I don't know. I asked her to make me a list of names for the kittens in my barn, but she hasn't shown it to me yet."

"Give her time."

Carrie scowled. "I don't know how much time I'll have with her. Ryan could take off at any moment, the way he showed up out of the blue."

Matt reached across the table and took both her hands in his. When their gazes met, he squeezed her hands reassuringly. "Ryan's done a good job so far. You said so yourself. Sam is happy and healthy and loved. It may be hard for you when they leave, but at least you know that about her now."

"I guess," she muttered with reluctance, but she did feel better. Matt had it right—Sam was all those things Carrie wanted her to be. Except she wanted her permanently living in Little Tree.

Matt took his dishes to the kitchen to thank Leo for the catfish Leo had saved for him. Back at the table, compostable to-go box in hand, he said, "Leo wants you to go home. Says he'll mop in the morning."

"You're a saint, Leo," she called to the kitchen. A gruff harrumph came in reply, making her chuckle.

"I'll see you home." Matt pulled open the door for her.

"Why? I mean, thank you, but it's out of your way."

"Someone might follow you."

She raised a brow. "Someone other than you, you mean?"

He laughed. "Someone whose intentions aren't so pure."

"Ri-ight."

"Besides, that's what a gentleman does at the end of the date. Make sure his lady gets home safely."

Matt checked up and down the street, and Carrie followed his gaze, wondering what he sought. She frowned at the one car she didn't recognize which sat down the block, away from any stores. Bars like Buck's and Kerr's Grill stayed open this late, and the gray, or maybe blue, sedan sat nowhere near either. Was that someone in—

Matt swept her into his arms. "I've been wanting to do this all night without Leo and the whole town watching."

She smothered a giggle as he set his mouth on hers. His muscles bunched as he held her even closer. His silky hair caressed her fingers as she returned his kiss.

Had Sam been able to fall asleep tonight without worrying about mice?

Carrie winced at the distraction and applied herself to the kissing. Making an effort must have shown because Matt loosened his hold and leaned back to look at her. "What's wrong?"

"Sorry. I'm sorry. I can't get Sam out of my mind."

Matt sighed. "At least it's not Winslow or some other guy."

She let out a surprised laugh. "Ryan? Are you kidding?"

"Might be easier." Before Carrie could follow up

on that remark, he added, "What's really bothering you, sweetheart?"

"Everything. Nothing. As you reminded me, she's fine, or at least has been up till now. But what about school? What about friends? What damage does it do to a kid not to have a permanent home?"

"Now, don't get mad, okay, but she has a home. With her dad."

Carrie scowled. "I know that."

"It might have wheels, but he's her security. And isn't that what home is?"

"But who takes care of her while he's practicing or competing?"

"Sounds like you have some questions. Unfortunately, I'm not the right person to ask." Matt drew her flush to his body again. "But I might be the right person for this."

He leaned into her again and Carrie let her cares float away. Because Matt was the *exact* right person for this.

CHAPTER THREE

Carrie returned home later than usual after her shift at the diner and making out with Matt. Pushing open the creaky truck door almost depleted her energy reserve. The customers had been demanding tonight, even her regulars. To be honest, they were all her regulars. But something like the full moon had strung everyone tight. Their fish wasn't hot enough, or they'd asked for their condiments on the side of the burger rather than on it, or the coffee tasted too weak or too strong. Piddly issues she usually kept on top of and wouldn't have let bother her.

Perhaps it simply capped off her rotten afternoon. She'd missed Sam and throughout the day had wondered what her niece was doing. After only one day home, the girl had dug under her skin.

When Ryan and Sam took the cats over to their place, Carrie had wandered from chore to chore, listening for their truck. She wanted to show Sam pictures she'd taken of Hannah and of Sam as a baby. She wanted to show her how to make hotcakes and cornbread. She wanted to take Sam shopping and buy her something pink. She wanted to form a bond and become someone important in the girl's life.

Nearing the house, Carrie heard male voices raised in argument. She quickened her step, worried Adam had brought home trouble. Even when she recognized the second voice as Ryan's, she didn't slow. Thank God Matt hadn't followed her home to witness this.

"You're a drunk," Ryan said in a rumble like an impending storm.

She yanked open the screen door to see Ryan leaning over Adam at the kitchen table. Her brother slouched in his seat, one boot heel on the worn rung of the wooden chair, the other leg stretched before him. Despite his lazy pose, his brown eyes had narrowed and one hand fisted at his side. She had to admire his restraint. No other man would dare speak to her six foot three brother, drunk or sober, with such disgust. The tumbler in front of him held clear liquid. She sighed with relief. Since Adam drank mainly beer or whiskey when he imbibed, this must be water. Thank you, Lord.

"You need to get your act together or get out," Ryan said. "Carrie doesn't need you screwing up—"

"How do you know what I need?" Carrie stepped into the fight. Her defense of Adam didn't take a second thought. "I can speak for myself."

Ryan glared at her. "I'm talking to your brother right now. Privately."

"It's so private I could hear you from outside by the truck."

"If he hadn't just fallen into the house, I would have had this talk in the morning."

Carrie scanned her brother again. He wore battered jeans, boots and a short-sleeved shirt that could be the one he'd had on the day before. Or not. It certainly looked wrinkled and dusty enough to be yesterday's. His chocolate brown hair could use a wash. When she inspected his face, he raised a brow.

She winced and mouthed "sorry," but not before noting his bloodshot eyes. He carried himself like a man bone-tired, not drunk, and she unfortunately knew the difference. But she couldn't guess what he'd been doing the night before. Often his binges led to three-day hangovers.

Nevertheless, he was her brother. "You can't yell at Adam like that."

"How do you want him to yell at me?" Adam gave her a half-grin.

She swiped her hand sideways to hush him. "This is none of your concern, Ryan."

"It *is* my concern. You're my family."

She scoffed. "Couldn't tell it by the way you've been acting."

"What's that supposed to mean?"

Carrie poked him in the chest. "Cutting us off from Sam, that's what."

He stepped back, his wide eyes indicating surprise rather than fear of her puny shot at intimidation. "I didn't cut you off. You did that yourself after Hannah died."

Adam shook his head. "I know that's not true. Carrie's worried herself sick over Sam."

Ryan frowned. "Why would you worry?"

How could he be so dense? "You disappeared

with her. I didn't have a phone number or email for you. I didn't know where you'd be competing. There was no way to get in touch or check on her."

"I thought you'd forgotten her."

Carrie gasped. "Are you crazy?"

"Never," Adam said. "She's our family."

"Okay, okay." Ryan held up his hands in surrender. "I made a mistake. But why would you worry? Do you think I can't take care of her?"

Carrie made a helpless gesture. "How could I know?"

"You could trust me. I do a damned sight better taking care of her than Adam does taking care of you."

"Hey, now." Adam rose from his seat.

"I don't need taking care of."

Ryan pointed at Carrie. "Yes, you do." He pointed at Adam. "No, you don't. Even I can see that, and I've only been here one day."

"No one asked you to butt into our business," Adam said.

"I'm family too. I'm also the oldest, so it's my duty to watch out for you."

Carrie shook her head. "That's ridiculous."

"It's true. So while I'm here, I'm going to help Adam get sober."

Adam blew out a breath, clearly exasperated. "I told you. Last night, I stayed out late with the guys, *drinking pop*, and I didn't want to wake up Carrie. I slept in the bunkhouse."

"You don't have to do that," Carrie said.

Adam shrugged. "This morning, I headed out with the men to tend the fence line. Had I known you'd *dropped in unexpectedly,* Ryan, I would have stopped at the house to say hello. To Sam."

Carrie grinned. She loved Adam standing up for himself almost as much as she loved his ability to stand up sober. Even though he claimed he hadn't had a drink in "a long time"—whatever that meant in his life—his absence last night had worried her. She felt guilty for doubting him when he struggled to stay on the wagon, but she'd been led down the path of gullibility before. It was why she slept with her phone charging on her bedside table and had the exact amount of cash for bail in the side pocket of her purse to bail him out of the drunk tank.

"Why don't we call it a night," she said. "Adam's home and I'm tired."

Ryan put his fists on his hips, wincing as he did so. "Just because he's not drunk this time doesn't mean he's reliable. I want to know what you're doing to stay sober, Adam."

Adam wasn't his responsibility. Not like—

"Where's Sam?" Carrie asked.

"Upstairs, sleeping."

She glanced toward the stairway, wondering how the girl had slept through the men's argument.

"She likes noise," Ryan said, reading her concern. "It's the quiet that freaks her out."

"Not that you're unwelcome—not that Sam's unwelcome anyway," Carrie corrected herself, "but why are you here? I thought you were determined to stay at Windy Glade tonight."

"You had to work late."

She waited. He didn't expand on his statement. "And?"

"I didn't know that Adam would be here." Ryan glared at Adam, no doubt driving home the message of Adam's unreliability. "I wanted to be sure you got home safely. There's no phone at my place, so we decided to take you up on your hospitality one more night."

Touched, she placed a hand on his forearm. The heat of the night shimmered off his skin. "Although your intention was sweet, I don't need anyone checking up on me. I'm a grown woman and I do perfectly fine when you're not here. Which is most of the time. Besides, Little Tree is the safest town on the planet."

"Even a safe town has its rotten apples. Some idiot might take it into his head to follow a pretty woman like you home."

She couldn't suppress a jolt of surprise at his casual compliment and snatched away her hand in reflex. What had gotten into the men in town? First Matt wanting to see her home safely, now Ryan. No one ever had to worry about her. "The ranch hands would—"

"The bunkhouse is too far away from the house for them to hear you scream. If Adam's not here or he's...*incapable* of helping you, you'd be vulnerable."

"There's a gun in my truck."

"There's a gun in every truck in the state. Some stalker would have one too." Ryan's mouth tightened. "I couldn't sleep without knowing you were safe."

Carrie stared into his eyes, noting his genuine worry on her behalf. She wasn't used to being the person causing anyone anxiety.

"You're going to have to give in on this one, Carrie," Ryan said gently but with steel determination underlining his words. "I can't stop caring about what happens to you simply because you're over twenty-one."

The intensity of his concern made her breath hitch. She had to swallow before she could speak and reached out for contact again. To reassure him that while she was grown and capable and his worry was needless and a little silly given he was never here, she wasn't blowing off his feelings. "Thank you for thinking of my well-being," she said softly. "It's not necessary but I do appreciate it."

"You don't have to thank me," he replied just as softly.

Neither said anything else, nor did they break eye contact. Carrie's heart pounded in her ears. Her mouth went dry. Heat rose in her face. She became aware of the silky masculine hairs under her suddenly sensitive fingertips. She stood close enough to feel his breath on her face. Close enough to watch his pupils dilate. Close enough to—

"Do you two want to be alone?" Adam said.

~~~

Ryan stepped away quickly, a frown and hard-eye turned toward Adam. "Don't be stupid."

Carrie had jumped back as though scorched by her brother's words.

"She's practically my sister," Ryan emphasized to the room. This place turned his head upside down. So many memories of his youth and of Hannah. Should he have taken her away to rodeo? Would she have been happier if they'd stayed on at Windy Glade with his parents, being near her own family?

He took a breath. Family. Right. These two stubborn Moores and Sam were all he had left. As the oldest, the responsibility fell on him to care for everyone in Hannah's stead. Even though he had to do it from afar, he owed it to her memory.

Since he had to recuperate at Windy Glade, he'd make sure the Moores were in good shape for when he eventually had to leave Little Tree.

He snorted to himself. Some guardian he was.

"I have to run into town tomorrow," Carrie said to him. "I'd like to take Sam with me if that's okay with you."

Whatever heat had been building in that weird moment between them had been effectively doused by her words.

"Why?"

Clearly exasperated, she blew out a breath. "For company."

"I'll have to think about it." Ryan turned to Adam, who held his hands up as though to ward him off. "Are you going along with them or working or whatever it is you do?"

"Don't start on me," Adam said. "I've got fences to tend to. And frankly, pal, you're family. But not the head of the family."

Ryan smirked with a challenge he knew would go unanswered. He needed to give Adam a wake-up call. "Who do you think is the head of the family then?"

Silence followed. Carrie hid her anguish by looking away from them.

Adam gave a sideways gesture with his head, indicating his sister. "She is."

"That's not tr—"

"Yeah, it is, Carrie," Adam said. "I work on the

ranch. You run it. You watch over the men and take care of the main house. Since Matt's been gone, I've tried to step in as ranch foreman, but the men all defer to you for directions. They know who runs this place. You make sure the bills get paid, though Lord only knows how some months."

"We're family, Adam," she said. "We both keep this place running."

Adam grinned and made as if to touch his hat brim. "Yes, ma'am." Then he turned and left the house.

Carrie glared at Ryan. "Now see what you did."

Surprised, he stepped back, hand to his chest. "What I did?" He eyed the door. "If he goes to get a drink because he's had to face a hard truth, that's his choice. You need to stop blaming others for what Adam does."

She pointed a finger and would have poked him in the chest again if he'd been close enough. "Ryan Winslow, don't you come in here and think you know anything about us. Do you think Adam is happy or proud of himself? Do you think he needs you to point that out?" She huffed out a breath. "Ask yourself this. In all the years your father ran your household, did he ever make you feel like a worthless human being just to prove a point?"

She turned sharply on her heel, and like her stubborn brother, left the kitchen. Left Ryan alone, shut out of their family circle of two.

~~~

Carrie smiled over at Sam in the truck cab beside her the next day as they headed into town. She wanted more of this: the simple everyday pleasure of having her niece beside her. Secure in the knowledge Sam was taken care of.

Even if she had to butt heads with her stubborn brother-in-law to make it happen. Really, one would think she'd meant to kidnap the girl and run away forever. A little devil smirked inside her head. If Carrie had any place to run to, she might consider it. A place away, with no responsibilities, with days upon days of fun with Sam. Take a...what was the word...*vacation*?

Oh, sure, Dorothy. Sail over the rainbow, perhaps? She snorted to herself at the idea. She'd taken a week last year in Billings she wouldn't call a vacation, since she'd attended Al-Anon meetings and met with a counselor. Before that? She'd had a weekend away two years ago when her friend's bridal party went to San Francisco for the weekend. An expensive jaunt she still felt guilty about.

The ranch was her responsibility and her pride. She kept it going for her parents and all the hundreds of years of Moores preceding them, and for the future. For Sam, if she wanted it.

She'd broach that subject with Ryan another time.

It had been hard enough to convince him to let Sam run to town with her for groceries. The men would come in for the order for the bunkhouse; Carrie only took home the month's groceries for the main house.

"You have a lot of chores," Ryan had challenged her when Sam ran into the house on a last-minute errand. "How are you going to watch Sam too?"

"As mothers through the ages have done," she'd shot at him. "Women are hard-wired to do more than one thing. We hunt, we gather, we tend children."

"She'll be in the way."

"She'll be a helper."

"I need her here."

"She'll be in your way." Carrie had smirked, she

remembered now with a hint of shame. Maybe not the best move, since his jaw had tightened. She'd rushed on. "You can borrow a horse to tour Windy Glade if you want. I mean, if you can ride."

Oops. Not only did his jaw tense but his eyes flared like a gas flame on a stove. Quick and hot.

"I. Can. Ride."

"And probably farther and faster without Sam. Or there must be other chores like checking the outbuildings where you'll want to watch for rotted boards. And snakes."

She let the dual images form in his mind and thought she'd seen him waver. He did, the result being a charming day alone with her niece.

"Aunt Carrie."

"Yes?"

"Is there... Could we..."

Carrie waited her out. Poor Sam had been cursed with both the stubborn Winslow genes and the Moore pride.

"I brought some money and I want to buy something." The words spilled from Sam in a rush.

"Sounds doable. What do you want to buy?"

"Is there a store for girls? Like, you know, hair

stuff?"

Shooting her a quick glance, Carrie noted the expertly braided hair and clean, though worn clothes. "You bet. We'll stop there before the grocery store so the ice cream doesn't melt."

Sam's head popped up, expression bright. "Ice cream?"

"What's your favorite flavor? I like all of them, except pistachio." Ryan's favorite, though why she remembered that was beyond her.

"I like them all too. I've had chocolate *and* vanilla."

Carrie tightened her grip on the steering wheel. Five years old and Sam had only tasted two flavors of ice cream? That was almost child abuse.

"Maybe we'll get a couple of different pints and have a tasting party."

Sam squealed, acting like a little girl without a care in the world. Tears pricked Carrie's eyes.

"Can we get one of pistachio too? Daddy says he likes it best, but I've never seen him eat any."

"Sure." Maybe the store stocked single serving cups, she thought sourly.

Little Tree boasted two stores with clothes, but

Carrie avoided the feed store, whose selection leaned toward sturdy clothing. Her friend, Lexi, had had bad dealings with them recently. Carrie didn't know all of the details, but until she had the whole story, she'd avoid the feed store out of loyalty.

The small "department store" carried everything one needed for everyday life. Prom dresses and suits required a trip to Billings or a mail order pickup. Internet order, nowadays. She walked into Annie's Store and nodded hellos to the other shoppers. Every person gave a double-take on seeing Sam at her side. Carrie ignored them. If they hadn't heard about Ryan's return, word would spread soon enough.

She headed to the girls' section. Carrie had shopped at Annie's with her mom, and her mom had shopped with Grandma. The original Annie had opened the store around 1929, just in time for the stock market crash and following Great Depression. That was how luck ran in Little Tree. The citizens hadn't had enough money to buy her goods, but Annie had owned the building, so she opened the doors to the citizens to socialize. The stock on the shelves barely changed for years.

Today, Carrie followed her niece as she

wandered past the jeans and shorts toward the pretty pastel dresses. Sam touched some of the soft fabrics as she passed, grasping a few with a faint smile. She didn't stop, though, until she came to the accessories. Hair ribbons. Pink hair ribbons.

Sam jammed her hand in her pocket and came up with a fistful of coins. She pointed at a card with different shades of pink ribbons on barrettes and opened her fist to show her fortune. "Do I have enough for that?"

The barrettes' price sticker read $4.99. Carrie added up the shiny coins and came up with $1.12. "I think so. Let's see what else there is here before you make a purchase."

The little girl's jaw hardened. "Yes, ma'am, I'll look. But that's what I'm buying."

Winslow stubbornness. "Fair enough."

She took down the card of ribbons. Sam held it fisted in her hand as they shopped. "Hmm," Carrie said as though just thinking of this, "do you remember getting a package from me for your birthday?"

She knew darn well she hadn't had an address for Ryan for the past two years. There hadn't been an opportunity to send anything.

"I don't remember," Sam muttered.

Hard feelings there. Carrie squatted to her level. "You move around so often from rodeo to rodeo, I don't have an address for you."

Sam's brown eyes widened and her mouth formed an "O."

"I remember your birthday every year, but I don't have a way to contact you. Or for Christmas." Carrie let that sink in. "Appears I'm a few presents behind."

"That's okay." Sam's fist full of money tapped her aunt's shoulder in comfort. "I don't need presents."

The statement almost made Carrie cry.

"But I need to give them," Carrie said. "It would make me happy to think you had something from me. Would you let me give you those presents now? Please?"

Sam frowned. "What would you give me? I have everything I need already."

While Carrie grappled with that staggering remark, Sam's gaze wandered to the dresses.

"Presents," Carrie said, "aren't always about need. I'd like to give you something simply because I want you to have it."

"Well…" Again, Sam's gaze strayed to the dress rack.

"And Uncle Adam asked if you'd pick out a couple of books you'd like."

"Books?" she whispered as though offered chocolate bars *wrapped* in pink hair ribbons.

"Books." Carrie turned to the clothes to hide her tears. "And a couple of sets of clothes."

"That's too much."

"Uncle Adam and I are several presents behind."

"I mean, it's too much to carry from rodeo to rodeo."

Carrie nodded, tamping down anger toward Ryan. "Then we'll limit ourselves to what fits in your duffel bag. Maybe you have some clothes that are too small that you need to replace soon."

A corner of Sam's mouth twisted as she wrestled with emotions. Doubt or confusion brought a frown to her eyes. "Maybe."

"Let's see what they have."

And shop they did. For almost an hour, Carrie made the girl try on clothes and pick out books and hair doodads. "This is tiny," she said, handing some soft-care elastics to Sam for her braids. "See how these will fit into your bag," she said, rolling up a half dozen pastel T-shirts. Cute shorts followed, in navy and emerald and yellow, the latter of which made Sam laugh like Ryan at his most cynical. "Oh, Aunt Carrie. How would I keep the yellow ones clean?"

The girl rejected half of what Carrie wanted to buy for her. She chose two books—one for a birthday and one for a Christmas gift—from Adam. "I couldn't have read them before last year," she reasoned, "so he wouldn't have given me books when I was a *baby*."

More barrettes made their way onto the checkout counter. "I have ribbon at home. I think we can make you some more." Or if not, she had a few friends who would know how.

Ready to move on to the grocery store, they walked over to check out.

"Hi, Ms Moore," the teenage shop clerk said before turning to Sam. "I'm Courtney. Don't know that I've seen you around."

"That's 'cause I travel the rodeo with my daddy, Ryan Winslow." Sam stood as tall as she could. "We own Windy Glade."

Courtney smiled. "Thank you for coming in to shop today at Annie's, Ms Winslow."

"I'm not old enough to be Ms Winslow. My name is...Sammie." The little girl slid a glance at Carrie, who smiled with a nod.

Oh boy, Carrie thought. Ryan would think she'd had something to do with this name change.

"I'm buying this." Sammie plunked down the original barrette card with her chin jutted out. She dug out her change again and cupped it upside down on the counter so none would spill.

"And I'm buying this." Carrie plopped her pile of clothes and the two books on the leftover space. She caught the clerk's attention and mouthed, "And that."

Courtney nodded.

"Let's see if you have enough." She counted out Sam's money while the child bit her lower lip. "Oh!"

Sammie tensed. "What's wrong?"

"Not a thing. I owe you..." She counted three pennies and a nickel into the little girl's palm. "Eight cents."

Sammie's mouth gaped.

Courtney put the barrettes in a bag and handed it across.

"Thank you," Sammie breathed out, clutching

the package to her chest.

"Thank *you* for shopping with us today. Come back soon." She turned to Carrie's pile and began ringing the items into the computer.

"Thanks," Carrie whispered as Sammie wandered not too far off.

"I have a sister, though she's a little older. I understand when a girl just needs something to make her feel better."

At that, Carrie recalled why she knew the clerk. The community had done a fundraiser for her younger sister and the family to pay for medical bills. "How is Daisy?"

Courtney beamed. "Great, thanks. She's in remission" —three knocks to the wood counter— "and she's as sassy as an eight-year-old should be, thinking she owns the world. Though my parents may have something to do with her having that attitude."

Carrie laughed with her. She'd email the owner later and let him know what a caring and personable employee he had.

"The boss asked me to mail this today, but I may as well give it to you." Courtney extended a letter-sized envelope to Carrie. "Payment for your postcards. He said he'd email you which ones he wants restocked."

"Oh, that's great." She'd left a few of her original photo postcards at Annie's and at the Catch-All on consignment. Her share of the sales wouldn't pay for Sam's barrettes, but the postcards kept her name and images in front of people who might need to hire her for portraits. She worked with a photographer in town for larger events but hadn't had many bites for individual work since prom season.

Grocery shopping took another hour as Carrie tried to coax Sam into making selections. What vegetables did she like or dislike? Honey wheat bread or multi-grain? Chicken or pork? Through it all, Sam only shrugged. Carrie didn't know how to translate the gesture. Did her niece not have a preference, did she eat everything, or had she not tasted many of the choices offered? The budget didn't stretch to extravagancies, so Carrie bought what she had on the list, earning a nod from Sam—er, Sammie every time she asked if the choice suited her.

Small steps, she reminded herself. She'd learned a lot more about Sammie during clothes shopping and lost a little ground in the food aisles. She'd take the day as a win.

Sammie pitched in loading the groceries in the truck without having to be asked or directed, clearly familiar with the task. Carrie grudgingly gave Ryan points for teaching the child both manners and responsibility. And Sammie hadn't fussed with how long shopping took or whined or begged for treats. More points for Ryan.

Carrie didn't want to learn he'd been a bad parent. But if he had a few faults, it would help her to convince him to leave Sam with her for schooling come September, an idea that grew stronger with every precious moment she spent with her niece.

~~~

Ryan strode to the house from the barn, glad no one had seen his painful dismount of the gelding he'd borrowed to ride over to Windy Glade. His shoulder hurt like a son of a bitch, and he could hardly wait till he tucked Sam in tonight so he could have a pain pill.

Some father he was.

If Adam hadn't been around the Moore house, Ryan would have downed enough whiskey to feel no pain but still be able to respond if Sam had a nightmare. But he couldn't exactly lecture Adam for numbing his pain in a bottle if he planned to do the same.

Come to think of it, Ryan didn't know the reason Adam drank. Had he lost someone he loved deeply, other than his parents and sister? Or were their deaths enough to tip Adam over the edge? Did there have to be a heartbreak or even a setback to drive a man to alcohol? Had his genetic switch simply flipped on its own?

Still pondering the problem, Ryan ran an assessing eye over the barn. It had been sufficient for the horses used on a cattle ranch, but if he turned it into a bronc operation, he'd have to rebuild. Probably couldn't just add on, either. This place would have to be razed and a new barn raised. He snorted. Not the R&R the doctor had recommended for his shoulder to heal.

The two ideas playing in his mind were to breed broncs for the rodeo or to bring in troublesome broncs and re-train them for ranch work. He was more of a rider than trainer, but having been raised to be a cattle rancher, he'd learned the basics of animal husbandry. Now he wished he'd been more attentive to his dad's teachings about ranching instead of fixating on bronc riding.

Either plan required money. The barns would have to be upgraded into stables, the corral fences rebuilt, and pastureland considered. All of which depended on him winning prize money at Nationals, because his current savings wouldn't swing it. Renting out Windy Glade this past year had about killed him emotionally, but it helped pay the taxes. Though no showplace, the house was livable, and when Sam got older, she wouldn't have to be ashamed to bring friends home. They could use a new couch maybe. But there was no sense in replacing it to sit idle in a rental until they moved home. Given the setback this injury caused him, that might be a few years now.

Carrie's truck pulled past the ranch headed toward her place. He'd have to pick up Sam soon.

He headed to the barn again, pocket notebook and pencil stub in hand.

~~~

Carrie turned as the door slammed behind Ryan. He didn't knock before entering, a sign he felt at home.

She couldn't decide how she felt about that. Sure, as family, she wouldn't want him to knock, anymore than she would expect Adam to. On the other hand, she didn't want him thinking he had a claim on the Moore ranch. That remark about being the head of the family still stung.

"Daddy!" Sammie launched herself at Ryan as though they'd been separated for a year. Was that normal? The girl had had a good time, or so Carrie had thought.

"See what I buyed at the store." She dragged him to the table and handed him her small bag.

He pulled out the card of barrettes. "These are pretty."

"I used the money I found under the bleachers. Buyed them myself." The girl radiated pride.

Carrie barely managed not to wrinkle her nose. She leaned toward Ryan and said from the side of her mouth, "Put some hand sanitizer in the truck."

Ignoring Carrie, he said to his daughter, "That's good thinking. Keep your hair under control."

"Now you don't have to worry about pulling my hair into braids anymore."

He grimaced at the comment and slid the card

into the bag, an eye on the other purchases. "And what's all this?"

"Christmas and birthday presents. See what I got." Sammie dug into the bag and brought out the two books. "These are from Uncle Adam, from when he missed my birthday and Christmas."

Ryan shot a glance at Carrie. "Is that so?"

She held his gaze, unflinching.

"I can read them at the libraries when you do computer stuff."

He grunted.

"And Aunt Carrie got me stuff too. Do you want to see? Daddy?"

Ryan turned to Sammie. "Of course, sport."

"It'll all fit in my duffel. See?" She pulled out the folded T-shirts.

Carrie watched as Ryan admired the purchases. Did he notice the lack of brown and the addition of dresses to the choices?

"Did you say thank you to your aunt?"

"She did," Carrie said. "There are jeans as well for the fall, for school. I hope you'll be home this Christmas or at least send us your address."

He scowled. "We usually go to New Mexico after

Nationals. I work at a ranch over the winter, training young kids who want to learn bronc riding. Earn some money, keep in shape."

Carrie raised a brow. "Do they have Wi-Fi?"

"I'm sure they do."

"Then I expect you to keep in touch. We have the same email we've always had, though my emails to you have bounced."

He looked away. "I might have changed servers."

"We do our computer work at the library wherever we are," Sammie put in. "Daddy takes me to get a stack of books and I get to look at them until he's done. Then Daddy reads me the ones I liked best."

"That sounds nice."

"Now he can read me my very own books." The girl beamed.

"Speaking of reading..." Carrie started in a gentle tone, ignoring how Ryan stiffened. "Did you make that list of kitten names we talked about?"

Sammie's gaze slid away. "Not...yet. I could just tell you what I thought of."

"I'd rather see the list when it's ready." Carrie wanted to assess her writing. "I have paper if you want to work on it now."

"I have to put away my things." Sammie scooped her purchases into the bags. "I probably got chores at home too."

~~~

Ryan winced. Sure, there were chores, but a kid should be a kid sometimes. Especially at five. "I brought the cats back over this morning. Why don't you put that stuff in the truck and go see to the kittens in the barn. Make sure they're not missing you."

Sam's face lit. "Thanks, Daddy."

He watched her scamper off and made a mental note to make sure she had playtime. Not that she slaved away or anything, but he needed to see to it she did something other than chores.

"Thanks for taking her shopping," he said to Carrie. "I'm sure she enjoyed it. But you shouldn't get her so many presents."

"Why not?"

Because I can't afford to. What a crappy reason to deny his daughter anything. "I don't want her getting spoiled."

"That little girl is so far from being spoiled, it's

laughable. I had to force her to choose something I could buy for her."

He'd noticed all the presents came in pinks and light colors. Now that Carrie had confirmed those had been Sam's choices, not hers, he had to face the truth. He'd bought Sam clothes in easy-to-care-for colors, much like his own. One load at a laundromat made sense time-wise and money-wise.

Had Sam wanted girly colors all along or was this a new yearning? He sighed, knowing why she hadn't brought up her change of heart. Lack of money had led to lack of expectation. It killed him to think his little girl denied herself anything, wouldn't even ask for things she wanted. He was the worst parent.

He wanted to grab Sam from the barn and take her to town and buy her the whole storeful of pink and frilly stuff. But... He couldn't afford to do it. He had to swallow his resentment against Carrie.

"I'm sure she enjoyed the trip," he forced out— about the closest he could come to thanking her.

"I wouldn't have to buy her so much at once if I saw her more often," Carrie continued. "Or if I at least had a place to send presents. But you don't keep in touch. I don't know your riding schedule."

Jesus, not now. Already feeling like a crappy parent, he turned a glare her way. "You keep harping on that."

"It wouldn't bother you if you didn't know it was true. That's your conscience poking you."

"I'm pretty sure it's you poking at me."

"You know Hannah wouldn't have wanted you to keep Sammie from us. If you didn't feel guilty, it wouldn't matter what I said."

"Were you always this hard?"

Her shoulders fell, along with her expression. Carrie took a step back and sighed. "Probably not. But you can't be soft and run a ranch."

Dammit. He stood and put his hand on her shoulder. "Sorry. I shouldn't have said that. It's not true."

"It's a little true."

"You should make Adam help you, you know. It would be good for him to have some responsibility."

"He does." She slid from under his hand as she took a sidestep. "Maybe the pressure would be worse for him. Each alcoholic is different. I'd rather be working the ranch as partners, but I don't want to put too much on him." She narrowed her eyes. "And you're changing the subject."

"No, I'm not. We're talking about you and how the ranch work has made you tougher."

"Growing up made me tougher. Losing my parents and my sister. And you keeping Sam— Sammie away. That hurts."

"I'm not keeping her away from you on purpose." Ryan blew out a breath, exasperated. "I work somewhere else. My daughter goes with me."

"About that."

Dread knotted Ryan's gut. "About what?"

"About Sammie going with you."

He crossed his arms and glared at her. "Don't."

"I haven't said anything yet."

"Doesn't matter. The answer's no."

Carrie smirked. "Well, maybe my question had been 'is everything all right on the circuit?' So 'no' seems about right."

"Don't get smart."

"I am smart, Ryan. I went to school. Like Sammie should."

"I'm not arguing. And stop calling her Sammie."

"Seems like arguing. And she prefers that name." Carrie held up a hand. "She introduced herself as

Sammie to the salesclerk."

He blinked, taken aback. "She did?"

"It was so cute. She puffed out her little chest, saying she was your daughter and you two own Windy Glade."

He could imagine it. "The girl's not shy."

Carrie laughed. "No, she's not. She stood up real tall, at least for her size, so proud, and said how she worked the rodeo—" Carrie's eyes widened. "How she owned the ranch with you, I mean."

He couldn't help the smirk. "Bragging about loving the rodeo circuit, was she?"

Carrie shrugged. "Poor kid had been so dazzled by the pinks and purples she didn't know what she said."

"Why can't you admit she has a good life with me? I know the rodeo circuit can be difficult with a child, *for* a child, but I protect her. She's fed and cared for and loved. She has friends wherever we go."

Carrie touched a hand on his forearm for a moment. "Ryan, I've never doubted that you love her and take care of her."

When Carrie didn't say more, he relaxed. "Thank you. I think I needed to hear you say that."

"And she's turned out great so far."

Aw, dammit. "You just had to add that *so far*, didn't you?"

"She needs to go to school."

"Of course Sam needs schooling. And she's had it. There's a girl named Callie who teaches the kids. That's why Sam can almost read. She writes letters and numbers and does simple addition."

Carrie's shoulders fell. "Oh. That's good. I didn't know. She hasn't shown me her list of kitten names yet."

"She said she hasn't thought of the purrr-fect one yet." He smiled. "Her words."

"That's adorable." Carrie drew a deep breath. "Is Sammie at kindergarten level?"

Well, there went that eight seconds of accord.

"Jeez, I don't know. Probably. She knows her colors and can spell her name."

"Alert the Nobel committee," Carrie muttered.

"Look, she just turned five. She couldn't have gone to school before now anyway. And kindergarten is a perk, not even a requirement in most states. She doesn't have to be enrolled until first grade."

He hated the horrified expression on Carrie's

face. She made him feel like the worst father on the planet. He didn't need help getting there. Even he didn't believe, or maybe only half believed, what he was saying.

"You're not really going to make her skip kindergarten, are you?"

"I haven't decided." Or thought about it much, he admitted. His sights were set on training to win, winning to quit, quitting to build a permanent home for Sam.

"If there's really a *qualified teacher* on the circuit," Carrie said, "I'm sure Sammie will do okay with her school learning."

He blinked with surprise. All this build up leading to Carrie agreeing with his parenting? Had he missed something?

"However—" she continued.

Ah. Of course there'd be more.

"School isn't merely about academics. It's about learning respect through social rules like sharing and taking your turn and not cutting in line. Kids figure out how to maneuver through the world, deal with other people's demands and emotions, and manage conflict."

He scowled. "That's a lot for being five."

"And that's not all. She'll learn to separate from you, to be independent for four hours a day, and make decisions on her own. It's a time of growth."

"How do you know all this?"

"I've been thinking about it for about a year. Wondering what your plans are for her and her future. Wondering if you'd made any."

"All I do, I do for Sam."

"I know. Or I believe that, more now that you've come home."

"I'm going back."

Carrie took a deep breath. Ryan tensed.

"She needs a permanent home."

"She has me." He turned and stomped out, as mad at the truth of her statement as the impossibility of it.

He couldn't stop rodeoing now or he'd lose his sponsors. He wouldn't be able to convert the ranch into a money-making operation if he didn't win big this year. Then how could he provide for Sam if he lost their home to taxes? His New Mexico gig was seasonal, but he could probably work on someone else's ranch. That would give her a permanent home;

it just wouldn't be Windy Glade. He'd put everything into savings and had a tidy nest egg built up, but if he didn't have an income for the future, how would he feed and clothe her, let alone buy those damn pink hair ribbons?

CHAPTER FOUR

"Thanks for making time today," Carrie said to Matt as they reined in at the house with Sam alongside.

"My pleasure."

"Seriously, I know it's not easy to get a day off."

"Half day." Matt looked at her, held her gaze. "It was important we all" —he nodded to Sam— "spent time together."

With a smile, Carrie swung down and dropped Cooper's reins. She studied Sammie for discomfort, but the girl appeared more excited than sore. They'd kept the ride short for her sake. Carrie had given her a pink straw cowgirl hat before they set off for their ride, and Sammie had been beaming ever since. "How are you doin', peapod? You tired?"

Sammie shook her head vigorously and patted the gentle mare. "I like riding."

She leaned over into Matt's arms to be lifted down and Carrie stopped to take a photo. She'd been taking some great pictures all day. She made sure to secure the horse to the rail. Having borrowed the mare from Mike Torres, her tenant at the old homestead, she wasn't sure of the horse's training. Mike had assured Carrie the mare had been rehabilitated out of her bad habits and had gentle manners. She'd been a safe and easy ride for a little girl. Mike took in wild or abused horses, those no one wanted or could do anything with. He'd proven to be the horse whisperer his wife, Grace, claimed. Their leasing the old homestead with Mike's two younger siblings seemed to be working out, though Carrie didn't know how they managed space-wise. She thanked the heavens for their rent money and wished them continued success, both for them as her friends, and for the influx of funds to the Moore Ranch.

Sammie gave Matt an exuberant hug. "Thanks for taking me riding, Mr. Matt. I haven't been in a long time. Not since we had to give away Gus."

Her face fell. "Now we don't have a horse of our own anymore, but Daddy said Gus growed too old to go on the circuit with us. Now he's happier in a pasture where all he does is eat grass and sleep all day."

Carrie caught Matt's gaze. He gave a little shrug. She wondered if it was a nice explanation for a five-year-old but suspected old Gus had taken a really long nap in a pasture in the sky. She'd have to get details from Ryan.

With an arm around each of them, Carrie gave a squeeze. "That was so much fun today, but I'm parched. Who wants lemonade?"

"I do," Sammie said with a nod.

"Sounds good," Matt said. "Let me take care of your horses first. I'll take Mike's mare back to him and pick up my truck after some of your delicious lemonade."

"Thanks, Matt." She kissed his cheek as he set Sammie to the ground.

Sammie grinned at them. "Are you boyfriend and girlfriend?"

Matt nodded with a serious expression. "We are."

"I knew it," Sammie said.

Carrie kept her smile inside at his answer. They'd been dating for a few months now, and their relationship seemed to be working out. They had ranching in common, and she agreed with his views on life and the world. Their relationship rode along smoothly, and she felt a little thrill to hear him call her his girlfriend. They hadn't been intimate...yet. He'd become her dearest friend.

"You knew," Matt asked, "because your aunt kissed my cheek?"

"No, silly. Daddy said kissing doesn't hafta mean you're getting married. It's 'cause you and Aunt Carrie are always smiling at each other."

Carrie mulled that over as she and Sammie headed to the house to wash up. Kissing didn't mean marriage but smiling at someone did? She shook her head. She'd have to be careful who she smiled at.

Had Ryan had to explain this because Sam had caught him kissing someone? One of the "perfumed ladies?"

"Can I help?" Sammie asked. They'd gone into Carrie's bedroom to use her pink soap that Sammie liked.

"I'd appreciate it."

Once in the kitchen, Carrie handed down an unbreakable plate and a package of cookies to her.

Sammie arranged gingersnaps on the plate while Carrie poured lemonade.

"We make a good team."

The sound of boots being scuffed off on the mat came directly before the door creaked open. "Look who I found," Matt said as he entered.

Ryan came in behind him. He'd been at Windy Glade, doing who knew what. There was no sign of his sling, but he held his arm close to his side. She turned away before rolling her eyes. She wouldn't waste her breath trying to convince a cowboy to use good sense.

Sammie gave him a bright smile and a hug around his waist. "We went riding. I got to ride by myself."

"I saw you. You looked good up there."

Carrie hadn't known he'd returned to see them. Thinking about it now, she should have asked permission probably. But it hadn't occurred to her. She remembered Hannah teaching Sammie to ride when she was barely out of diapers. "We checked with Mike Torres for a safe mount for her."

"The mare looked good too." He nodded and washed his hands at the kitchen sink after Matt finished.

Why did she even keep soap and towels in the bathroom?

"It's been awhile, huh, sport?" he said.

She nodded. "I liked it. Can we go together?"

"If Aunt Carrie will lend us some horses."

They sat around the wooden table where Sammie chattered about the sights seen and fun had. Her joy of riding and appreciation of the Moore land at such a young age warmed Carrie's heart.

Matt set his empty glass on the counter and shook the crumbs from his cloth napkin over the sink before setting it alongside the glass. "Thanks for the cookies, and the day. I had fun with you ladies, but I should head back."

"Thanks for picking up the mare," Carrie said, "and returning her. Tell Mike I said thanks, and that she was the perfect mount."

"I will." He took a side-step to the door, hat in hand.

"Aren't you supposed to kiss her?" Sammie chirped. "'Cause she's your girlfriend?" She turned a laughing face to her dad. "I asked them, just to make sure, because they smiled at each other all day. And they kissed."

"I saw that, too." Ryan's gaze landed on Carrie.

Matt pecked her on the cheek, ice against her flaming skin, and she appreciated his restraint in front of their audience. Another man would have needed to stake a claim, and she'd have wanted to kick him in the shins for doing so. "I'll call you later."

She didn't care for the near-smirk on Ryan's face. His comment about being her protector and his attitude the night she'd worked late at the diner popped into her mind. He was neither her knight nor her big brother. "Wait. I'll walk you out."

Carrie took Matt's hand as they wandered to the barn. "Thanks for today."

He squeezed her hand.

"I appreciate you driving to the homestead to check out the gray for Sammie. Then giving her a test-ride over."

"Can't have your niece on an unproven horse, especially one Mike had to tame out."

Reaching the horse's side, Carrie slid into Matt's embrace. "You're sweet."

One side of his mouth quirked up. "Exactly what a man wants to hear."

Then he leaned in with a slow kiss that melted her bones. Sweet? Yeah. But also...dang hot.

~~~

Ryan watched the screen door bang shut after Carrie and Matt. He'd returned in the truck to find the house empty. Carrie had left a note on the kitchen table for Adam—who was who-knew-where—saying she and Matt had taken Sammie riding. That had given him a moment's pause. Should they have talked about it first? *Had* she mentioned it and he'd forgotten?

He'd swallowed the knot of fear that had risen. He trusted her with his daughter, knew Carrie would give her life to keep Sam safe. He'd lost Hannah to chuckwagon racing, a rodeo event she'd taken up instead of barrel racing after Sam came along. Hannah had won ribbons galore and some prize money. Not in the league with bronc busting or steer riding, but the money helped their family.

Then she was gone.

Just that fast, as he geared up for his own ride, he'd heard the crowd cry out, then the announcer. But he'd already been running, a pit in his gut, words of "overturned wagon" and "ambulance" not registering. The miracle was she'd died quick, before he even reached her.

So the idea of Sam on a horse without him took a minute to get used to. Didn't mean he didn't trust Carrie.

He'd been in the barn when he heard Sam's laugh and Carrie's voice, then some low male rumble that he figured must be the boyfriend. The former ranch manager here, who'd quit so he could date Carrie, if the locals at Buck's Bar were to be believed. *Romantic,* his ass. Sounded like he took in the lay of the land at Moore Ranch—Carrie, basically on her own, dealing with a couple hundred head of cattle—and set his strategy.

Ryan stayed out of sight in the barn in order to assess the guy. Rode well. Clean but not fussy or gelled up, which Ryan had seen when the guy swiped his arm over his forehead. Looked like a hundred other men in Montana. What did Carrie see in this one?

They stopped at the corral fence, where Carrie dismounted first and asked how Sam felt. Ryan's chest swelled when Sam didn't whine or complain, especially when he knew it'd been several months since she'd been atop a horse. Then... He had to swallow at the memory. The man had lifted Sam down, and his girl had fallen into his arms with open trust. The three had hugged and Ryan fought the ache in his throat. Sour like bile. After a minute, he realized it was envy.

The boyfriend had something Ryan wanted, though until he saw it played out in front of him, he hadn't known it. They'd appeared like a TV commercial of a happy family: father, mother, adorable kid. Happy and, if not prosperous, at least together. Settled.

He ached to think Sam didn't have that.

Dammit. He was trying. Maybe instead of putting off the renovations until he had the money he needed, he should come home this winter to Windy Glade and start what he could. It would be harder without his income from the bronc training job, but if he won enough the rest of this season, he could swing it. Give Sam a home, friends, an aunt and uncle nearby.

As the picture solidified in his head, he replaced Matt in the circle of hugs. The guy seemed decent enough. If he weren't dating Carrie, Ryan might even like him. Then it hit him. To make a similar family circle for his daughter, he'd have to start dating again.

And he just couldn't. Not yet. Even for Sam.

~~~

Carrie sped around The Diner, believing if she kept moving, she wouldn't notice how tired she was or how her knees hurt or think about how many things she should be doing at the ranch. The cattle had been moved to other grazing as the grass was depleted. She had a field growing grass to harvest and put away for winter feed, and she had access to the grass at Ryan's. How much longer would that continue? Another thing to talk to him about.

Fortunately, the lunch rush had passed, and she only had another hour before the dinner relief, a retired teacher named Beatrice, arrived. Lou had mentioned that Beatrice's feet had been aching from years of standing in front of a classroom. Carrie decided she'd worry about that another day, however, since the older woman hadn't called in sick.

She turned at the sound of the bell over the door chiming. A smile broke across her face, and in her insides, when she saw Matt. He pulled off his hat and sat at a table. "This your station?"

Carrie laughed. "The whole room is mine, cowboy. Sit anywhere."

She leaned forward for a kiss since the place was empty. "You here to eat or just see me?"

The flirtatious light in his eyes made her stomach feel like tiny goldfish floated in there, tickling her.

"You're the real draw, honey. That's why I came at 2:30, so the place would be empty. But if I could get a steak and salad, that'd cap off my visit."

"Men. Always thinking of food."

He caught her hand before she could turn away. "Not only food."

The fish swam as though in a hurricane.

She served him and refilled the other tables' condiments while he ate. After clearing his plates and bringing him coffee, she sat and just gazed into his eyes for a moment.

"What?"

Carrie shook her head. "You're just so handsome. I can't believe no one else snatched you up."

"They know I'm spoken for."

Her heart skipped a beat then raced as though he'd proposed. Some men needed flowers or candy to woo a woman. Matt only needed to be himself. Honest. Steady. Handsome didn't hurt, and he'd still be striking in seventy years, but his strong and true character shone through everything he did. She respected the heck out of him.

The door's bell dinged, breaking the connection. Which was just as well. Carrie couldn't be falling under the spell of Matt's eyes while at work.

A girl of about twenty entered, taking a seat at a booth by the wall. Her lightweight windbreaker struck Carrie as odd, given the August day had hit the nineties earlier. The girl hoisted a bulging backpack onto the seat beside her.

"Hello," Carrie said as she approached. "What can I get you?"

"Can I get a water for now?"

"Of course."

When Carrie returned with a large glass of water, the girl hadn't picked up the laminated menu. "There aren't any specials, so order whatever you want."

"I'm going to need a minute. And I'd, um, like to use the restroom. Is it okay if I leave my water here to hold my spot?"

Carrie lifted her brows, then indicated the all-but-empty diner. Only Matt occupied a table. "I'll watch it for you."

"Thanks." The girl hoisted the heavy-looking backpack, bulging with who-knew-what, onto one shoulder and plodded to the restroom.

Carrie shook off the niggle she felt under her breastbone and returned to Matt. They talked about work at each ranch.

When the girl returned after almost fifteen minutes, Carrie went over to take her order. The girl looked better. Refreshed. While trying to figure out why she thought that, Carrie noticed the pink T-shirt the girl wore had WYOMING spelled across the chest. The "O" had horns that in no way resembled a cow, but whatever. She felt pretty sure she'd have noticed it before. The other shirt had been...a light green if she recalled correctly.

"Have you decided?"

"Sorry, I didn't look at the menu. I'll have a small milk to start." She moved a strand of light brown hair off her shoulder. The hair caught the light and seemed a shinier brown with red undertones. A dark patch on the girl's shoulder made Carrie study her again. The girl's hair appeared damp.

Ah. She'd washed her hair and changed her shirt in the restroom.

Carrie brought her a large milk.

"Sorry, I'm still deciding."

"No problem. Let me know when you're ready." Carrie returned to Matt while the girl "decided." From the corner of her eye, she noticed the girl pouring her glass of water into a water bottle taken from her backpack. A sinking feeling hit her stomach. She leaned toward Matt.

"Can you stay for a couple more minutes? I might bring you some eggs."

"I can stay, but I just ate a huge steak, as you know. What's going on?"

"I'll eat the eggs, okay, but you'll sit here?"

"I can make that happen."

She stood and going past him, pecked his cheek. "Thanks for not asking."

Carrie approached the girl's table. "Decide on what to order?"

"I'm not sure I'm going to order. Is it, um, okay if I drink my milk and sit for a while?"

"Of course." Decision made, Carrie slid into the booth across from her, ignoring the widening of her light brown eyes. "Hey, could you eat some eggs? I made the order wrong. That guy" —she indicated Matt with a jerk of her head— "wanted them cooked one way and I screwed up. He won't eat them. Now they'll have to go to waste. No charge, and you'd be doing me a favor. The boss hates to see food in the trash."

Which wasn't a lie. Lou did grouse about people ordering and not finishing their food.

"Well..."

"Please say yes. Unless you're a picky eater like my other customer. How do you usually like your eggs?"

"Honestly? Any way they come, but—"

Carrie beamed at her. "Thank you. So much."

She jumped to her feet before the girl could catch her breath. She hurried to the kitchen, swinging through the door. "Lou, I need a favor. Eggs, really fast, and you can choose how you cook them. I'll make the toast."

The old man didn't so much as blink before pulling two eggs from the refrigerator. "Meat?"

Carrie hesitated, not sure if she could pull that off, then decided to go for it. After all, it was more believable that a man with Matt's build had ordered meat. "Bacon, I think."

One bushy gray eyebrow rose. "You think?"

She popped some whole grain bread into the toaster. "I'll need a second order of eggs, any way but the way you're making these. Let's say scrambled since I'll probably wind up eating them."

Lou grunted. "Meat?"

"Bacon again. She won't check that closely and I don't want sausage. This'll be my lunch before I leave."

Carrie popped in two pieces of white bread with a grimace. Not her favorite, but toast would be pretty visible across the room. Had to sell the story.

She buttered all four pieces and plated them separately with some jellies.

"Order up." Lou caught her eye. "You planning to tell me what's going on in my diner?"

"Hungry stranger. Only ordered milk."

Lou grunted and turned to the stove. "Scrambled will be done before you can get back in here."

"Thanks, Lou." Carrie swung open the door with

her rear as she'd done since high school and turned a one-eighty into the dining room. She set the plates on the girl's table.

"I didn't know it came with bacon and toast."

Carrie heard the near-panic in the girl's voice. She made her tone quiet. "I wrote 'wh' and the cook made whole wheat. But I write 'w-w' for whole wheat and 'wh' for white. Maybe Mercury is in retrograde or something."

"What?"

"You know, when the world gets messed up."

"Then it must be," the girl said. "So there's no extra charge?"

"Miss," Matt called from across the room. "Is the chicken done laying my eggs yet? I can't wait all day."

Carrie laughed, then blanked her expression. After rolling her eyes for the girl, she turned toward him, no longer hiding her smile. "It'll be right out, sir."

"I would hope so."

She leaned toward the girl. "Thank you. And like I said, no charge for any of it. You're doing me a favor. Gotta go."

Before the customer could object, Carrie rushed

off. In the kitchen, Lou said, "Matt need to enroll in acting school? 'Cause he ain't that convincing."

"Ad-libbed, and he was awesome." She took the plates to Matt's table.

"Milk?" He made a slight tilt of his head toward the girl.

"Yes, sir."

"That's much better service. You might get a tip after all."

She pressed her foot onto his boot. "That's so considerate of you, sir."

He grinned.

She returned with a carafe of cold milk and a glass for Matt. After pouring his, she took it and the water jug to the girl. Her plate had been scraped clean and only a corner of toast remained. Carrie refilled her milk glass.

"I didn't order more milk."

"Refills are free." Carrie filled the water as well. "You let me know if you need something else. I'm going to go sweet-talk that guy some more. He might be a picky eater, but he's kind of cute."

Carrie sat by Matt with her back to the girl's table. "Don't say anything if she gets up and leaves.

I told her it was free."

"She's a little old to be a runaway. Twenty maybe. Younger than Bryce."

Carrie knew Matt's younger brother seldom kept in touch. Bryce had gone to college and taken a job in Bozeman, near enough to visit, though he didn't. Matt had told her his brother had fallen for a girl and had no time to introduce her, which Matt thought meant it wasn't serious. Carrie had other, darker opinions about the way Bryce treated Matt.

"I think she's hungry." Carrie took a fork from her apron pocket and snagged a bit of scrambled egg. "I like ketchup on mine."

Matt grimaced and squirted a dollop beside the hot sauce he'd poured on his plate. "That's no way to eat eggs."

"I usually like salsa, but I don't want another trip to the kitchen make you appear too cranky. You're already a picky customer."

"But cute. I heard you say so."

"So cute," she agreed.

He leaned forward and whispered, "I'll pay for the eggs, yours and hers."

Carrie shook her head. "I've got it, but thank

you."

"You don't look like a Rockefeller."

"I can cover her eggs, especially at employee discount rates. Which, with Lou, is very close to free."

"Doing your good deed for the day?"

"Maybe I'm simply hedging my bets for the future. Someday I might be hungry and broke, and I'll need someone to buy me dinner. It might even be her doing the buying. So, I take care of her today, and she remembers this kindness in the future. Maybe doesn't remember me."

He shook his head. "You'll hardly be recognizable in those rags you'll be wearing."

Carrie thought of the girl washing up in the restroom. *Bath*room for sure, in her case. "So, I'm actually watching out for myself."

"Right. Well, finish up, Mother Teresa. You have a table to clear." When she peered at him questioningly, he said, "Your diner just dashed."

Carrie's shoulders fell with disappointment but not surprise that the girl hadn't said goodbye or thank you. She felt bad for anyone to be in such straits and finished the scrambled eggs. At least she wouldn't have to cook herself dinner later. She walked over to clear the other table. When she got there, the girl had stacked her plates. And on the far side, sitting on the napkin where the girl had written "Thank You!" sat a dollar bill. Tears pricked her eyes.

She snatched it up and spun toward Matt, holding the napkin and money aloft with a big grin. "She left me a tip."

CHAPTER FIVE

Ryan thought to knock before walking into the Moore Ranch house that evening after he and Sammie ate dinner. He'd had a full day digging out small trees and shrubs that had taken root in what had once been a corral and hopefully would be again. He wanted to put Sammie to bed and take at least an ibuprofen. Another damn pain pill. He thought he'd be done with those by now, but his shoulder hadn't eased up. Probably because he had been working like a cowboy rather than a rodeo rider. Different muscles. The rodeo doc hadn't said to sit idle, but neither had he suggested clearing land.

Carrie opened the door with a smile, giving Sammie a hug before the girl scampered into the house. Carrie turned away and let the wooden screen door almost bang into him before he caught it. He narrowed his eyes. Great, she was in a mood. Right when he planned to ask her for a favor.

"I bought you some Country Blush soap," Carrie said. When Sam squealed and clapped her hands and jumped around like she had pogo sticks on her shoes, he had to bite back his objections. It's only soap, he reminded himself through his simmer.

But the purchase underlined another thing he hadn't bought for his daughter. The girl who never asked for anything. And now to keep her happy, he'd be special ordering a long-distance bar of soap so their place could smell like Hannah every time he inhaled.

Just great. Could his life get any more frustrating?

Maybe in actuality, the purchase underscored what a mistake coming home had been. He should have healed up in Deadwood or in some cheap-ass motel. Anywhere but home. Such as it was.

"I bought some fresh crayons," Carrie said. "You want to color in the living room while me and your dad talk?"

Dammit, he thought as Carrie produced a new

coloring book of that cartoon movie he hadn't taken Sammie to see. He should have bought her some crayons, at the least. Hers had become broken nubs, and she'd never asked for others. It simply hadn't occurred to him. Carrie's thoughtfulness pointed out where he lacked in parenting. And she wasn't even a damn mother.

Ryan caught himself swearing and realized he was the one in a mood. He hated to ask for a favor, especially something for himself.

He'd run into an old classmate who invited him to his wedding on Saturday. Ryan pointed out the late add-on, but Ted assured him the bride wouldn't mind. They'd planned an outdoor wedding and reception on his family's ranch. There would be plenty of food.

"What's one more?" Ted had said with a grin before abruptly sobering. "Or two? I mean, sorry. Wasn't thinking. Bring someone if you want to."

A vision of Carrie had popped into Ryan's mind. He'd recoiled sharply, as though he'd put his hand too near a stove burner. That'd be like a date. With Carrie. His dead wife's sister.

And yet...

She'd be the only woman he could imagine taking. The only woman he could picture dancing with. Laughing with. Talking to. Taking home.

He winced.

No. Just no.

His slight enthusiasm for getting out and seeing old friends at the wedding faded. He'd be better off staying home.

But attending the reception would enable him to establish contacts with other Little Tree ranchers. The old-timers could view him as an adult, and he would meet the newcomers or grown kids like Ted now in charge of their family ranches. He could talk horses, maybe get an insight which way to go with Windy Glade. Bringing in rodeo broncs to tame out might be tricky. Bringing in horses to breed for bronc riding, the same. He could keep Sam safe either way, but which would prove more profitable?

Going to an event brought its own problems and brought him to Carrie.

Once she came into the kitchen, Carrie leaned against the large white porcelain sink and crossed her arms, eyebrows raised. "What's on your mind?"

He forced the words out. "I came to ask for a

favor. Ted Rodriguez invited me to his wedding to Lisa."

Carrie smiled. "About time for them, wouldn't you say? They've been dating as long as you and Hannah were together."

"Teddy wanted to own his family's land so he'd have something to offer. And let her stretch her wings."

"Yeah, and she almost left Little Tree because she didn't think he was willing to commit."

"You know a lot about them."

"Waitressing is like being a bartender or a priest. People bring in their problems." She shrugged. "Sometimes it's slow. Lisa would come in on purpose during slow times to talk. I'm just far enough outside her circle of friends that it wasn't awkward to talk about personal stuff. And now, I'm inside the circle."

"Oh. So" —he cleared his throat— "you're probably going to the wedding."

She nodded. "As a guest but I'm also the back-up photographer."

"Really? I remember you taking pictures all the time, but I didn't realize you'd turned professional."

"It's hardly a living, not around here, and not

with my ranch work, but it helps with the bills."

"And you love it." He could see it in her expression when she talked, even this briefly.

Carrie shrugged and said again, "It helps with the bills. I can't do it full-time, and like I said, there's hardly a need in Little Tree for another photographer. So I hired on with Kent's Kandids as a helper. He lets me freelance. I take graduation or family photos a lot. I'll go onsite to people's farms, which Kent can't manage anymore."

Ryan slid into a straight-backed wooden chair at the kitchen table. "He was pretty old when he did my graduation photos a dozen years ago."

When she smiled her eyes softened, and she looked like someone a guy would want to snuggle up to. He only noticed because she didn't usually come off as approachable, let alone huggable. The difference had drawn his mind in that direction. That was all.

"I loved those shots, though. When I saw his photo of you and Hannah by that tree out back of Windy Glade, with your arms around her, I knew I wanted to take pictures like that. To try to capture peoples' feelings as well as their images."

"Really? I would have thought the bug hit when your picture of Hannah racing got printed in the rodeo program."

She laughed. "I'd just turned twelve then. Had a hard time deciding between being an astronaut or an environmental engineer. Because they'd both come in to talk to our school that year, remember?"

"The engineer got sick, so only the astronaut came to the high school. I was so focused on rodeo, I didn't care about other opportunities." He cleared his throat, pushing away old memories. "Anyway, about a babysitter."

"Sorry. I can't."

"Do you know a teenager I could trust?"

"Well..." She drew a breath. "He's not a teenager, but how about Adam?"

"Adam?" he echoed.

"He's not going to the wedding."

"Because of the temptation of alcohol? And you want him to babysit Sam?" Ryan snorted. "Yeah, I don't think so."

"That's not why he's not going. It would be good for Adam to believe you put that much trust in him."

"But would it be good for Sam?"

"To get to know her uncle? Yes. That's why you came home, isn't it? So if something happens to you—something *else*, Sammie will know us before she comes to live here."

"What makes you think that was my reason?"

Carrie rolled her eyes. "Doesn't take a genius, Ryan. You stayed away for two years, not even providing a cell phone number or email address. Then all of a sudden, you appear *after* you've been hurt? C'mon. Give me some credit."

He heard the edge in her voice. His disappearing act had hurt her. "I couldn't face either of our ranches without Hannah. I see her everywhere. Our two places and Little Tree are too full of memories. At first it was hard enough to see her likeness in Sammie every day. And I considered it a blessing at the same time."

She opened the oak upper cabinet and returned with two tumblers into which she poured Scotch. He inhaled and tried to shake off the memories. But he wasn't done yet. He took a bracing mouthful of the whisky, savoring the smooth comfort before continuing with his confession.

"I don't have any money to spare on internet

service, a computer, or a cell phone contract. That's why we go to libraries to use the public computers, to keep in touch with promoters and scheduling and all that. Hook up to the Wifi there for free."

He gritted his teeth against his humiliation and forced himself to continue. "I was using my friends' computers when I was on the circuit and didn't want to be social on their time. I kept it strictly to business emails. I started to worry I was imposing, so we began to use the library wherever we were." He sighed. "I'll get you my email address. And I'm going to apologize now for being an ass and not giving it to you before."

Carrie stared at him, and he felt both proud of himself for the apology and about two inches tall for having had to make it.

"Thank you," she said.

That simple declaration had him swelling and shrinking again. It meant so much to her and he'd withheld his frigging contact info—her lifeline to Sammie. Dammit. Hannah would have bullwhipped him.

Hannah. He sighed, his shoulders drooping.

Ryan ran a hand through his hair. "We used to

talk about coming home," he said quietly. "But in the terms of 'someday.' Ten years in the future, or when I aged out of bronc riding. Or if something happened to one of us."

"As a last resort."

Her dull tone and flat-eyed pain made him rush to say, "As a safety net."

"Same thing." She took a sip of her whisky.

"Not at all. Everyone needs a soft place to land." He stopped and quirked a half-smile. "Even bronc riders."

She chuckled. "You don't get much of that."

"Not during competition, that's for sure, but I've always considered Windy Glade my soft place. A haven, I guess. And an eventual destination."

"Good to know."

"I know what you're thinking, and it hurts to say it. I'm the reason Hannah never made it, never came back to her soft place. She'd been content—no, happy to follow me. She had barrel racing then chuckwagon racing. She made herself busy."

"She made herself a life on the circuit, Ryan, because you were there."

He stared into the amber liquid in his glass. "I

know."

Carrie's hand covered his on the table. "Because she loved you."

"I know." He reached for the bottle, more to move from her hand comforting him than because he wanted a refill. He didn't deserve comfort, and not from Hannah's sister. He topped off her drink as well. This next bit might go down smoother with the Scotch. Or enable him to say it.

He gulped, feeling the burn down his throat. It didn't actually help, especially since he hadn't let the whisky "finish" its job.

"Hannah never pushed for home because she knew I wanted to continue riding. I wanted to win the buckle." He fought down the sting behind his eyes. If only they'd come home, she would have had her family around her. She wouldn't have been competing or exhibiting.

She wouldn't have died.

"I'm sorry for that, Carrie."

"She could have been hit by a car, thrown from a horse, stricken with an illness. You don't control the world or the fates, Ryan."

He sent a sideways glance her way, a clutch to

his stomach. "How can you forgive me? I was hellbent on getting that buckle, on having my name on people's lips, on *fame*." He spit the word.

A sharp bark of laughter had him whipping his head toward her.

"Here's the thing, Ryan, and I can't believe you don't know this. Hannah loved you. She loved your life together, whatever life that would have been. You and Sammie were her sun and moon, and the rest didn't matter. She would have followed you to" — Carrie threw up her hands— "I don't know, some frozen star and made a home. As strong a person as she was, as certain in her choices, she'd fallen under your spell. She only ever wanted you, since about she turned nine and noticed boys."

He had to say it. "I loved her."

"I know. And thank you for that, because it made her whole to be with you."

He tilted the glass on its base, watching as the liquid slid one way then the other, catching the dim kitchen light from the sink across the room. "I'm not doing that anymore, just so you know. Chasing the buckle and the fame. I'm in it for the money."

She took a sip and studied him over the rim.

"I'm saving what I can. Hopefully this year, or maybe two more now that I've had to take time off, I'll be able to retire. Come home. Build something at Windy Glade. A horse ranch."

"That—" Carrie cleared her throat. "That would be great."

"We used to talk, Hannah and I, about what to do if something happened to one of us." He grimaced. "We meant me."

"Of course. The more dangerous profession."

"So you'd think. Bad fall, kick to the head, stomped on."

"But it was her."

"In an exhibition." Ryan sighed, thinking of the waste of a beautiful life. "She liked chuckwagon racing though. Became good at it."

"I know."

"Anyway, the thought had always been to bring Sam to Windy Glade. To build something there for her and our other kids." Pain speared him between his eyes, and he pinched the bridge of his nose to stave it.

"It was supposed to be *her* coming home, with or without me."

Carrie took another sip. She nodded as though making a decision, then took a deep breath. "I'm glad you came home. Even if you can't stay for long, even if we're a last resort."

"Never that." He put his hand on hers and squeezed. "You're a dream destination."

Her smile pulled him in.

He carefully took his hand away and grasped his glass, gaze fixed on its depths of color. "Hannah used to talk about me finding another woman if something happened to her. Not to be lonely, not to let Sam go motherless. But I couldn't imagine being with anyone else."

"I'm sure you told her to find happiness again too."

He snorted a laugh. "Hell, no. I wanted a shrine built to my memory, and her pining for me."

"That's probably what she would have done. But, Ryan, that doesn't make it right. Not right for you or for Sammie."

"She'll be fine. I mean, it would be ideal if Hannah were still here, but plenty of girls grow up okay without a mother. And she'll have you. I promise, we'll be home this year—" He thought of the money lost while he healed. "Or in the next few years, and we'll be back to stay."

Carrie stood, taking her glass to the sink. She carefully rinsed it, giving herself time to calm. Facing the sink, she said, "You can't drop into our lives and then disappear again. It's not fair to any of us, including Sammie. She has to get to know us all over again, every time."

A swirl brought her around, hands braced behind her on the sink edge. "And I may not be here, Ryan, standing around waiting for you to wander back to Little Tree. I might marry someone, move away. You can't count on me to raise Sammie if you wait for years or just drop in now and then."

A surprising dart of anger speared his chest. She was getting *married*? Leaving the Moore Ranch? It came as a punch to the gut and he responded without thinking. "I never asked you to *raise her.* But ever since we pulled up at home next door, you've been at me to stay. Now you're saying you're not going to act like a good aunt, that you're not going to be there for her? That's fine. We don't need you."

Red-faced with anger of her own, Carrie leaned forward, hanging on to the counter as though it kept her from launching herself at him. "I'm not so sure about that."

"Oh yeah?" Inside, Ryan shriveled. The playground comeback showed his lack of solid ground for this argument. But how dare she badger him about Sam's schooling, about life on the road for a young girl, and on and on, then snatch away her support? If she didn't really care about them, what was all that needling about? Just to rile him?

Because she'd succeeded.

He'd grown damn sick and tired of seeking her approval. And falling short in her regard. Why the hell did he care what she thought of him anyway?

He searched through his memory of conversations for a reason behind this sudden change of heart—because that's what it seemed like to him. At that phrase, *change of heart*, he got it. She didn't want to be a substitute wife and mother. She had her heart set on the real thing. It pricked him that he came in second-best to some cowboy. "So, it's serious between you and Matt Reynolds?"

Carrie drew back, blank faced. Was she surprised he'd figured out her plans? She'd mentioned getting married.

"You're going to go be a ranch foreman's wife now? The Olsteen place isn't that far away, you know. You could continue to see Sammie, if you really *wanted* to." He sneered, unable to keep from acting like an idiot, even though he heard himself doing it. "I guess your refusal to help out reveals your true feelings."

"*How dare you.*" She growled like a wild animal— or a frustrated woman. Rage reflected in her eyes. "I love Sammie," she continued in a more moderate tone. "You're keeping her away from us, not the other way around. But you can't have it both ways, Ryan, not being here but expecting us to wait for you. Life doesn't work like that."

As he well knew. What *had* worked out for him in the past two years? Hannah had been taken suddenly, cruelly, unfairly. He had to raise a toddler who'd become a school-aged child, and now he had to figure all that out. He'd scrimped to save money and had the worst fall of his career, creating a setback of unknown length.

Yeah. He knew all about life not working out as planned.

Unable to have this fight with Carrie, not seeing

it go anywhere productive, he walked out into the night. Once he cooled off, he'd go back in for Sam and get them both away from here.

~~~

The next day, Carrie diced vegetables she'd bought at an organic farm. It couldn't hurt for Sammie to have something natural for lunch—God only knew what she ate on the rodeo circuit. Ryan had had the gall to bring Sammie over for her to watch, and while she'd wanted to chase him off with a shovel, she'd never turn down any time with her niece. And honestly, she knew how hard it had been for him to ask after their argument.

She watched Sammie from the corner of her eye. The girl sat at the kitchen table with crayons and paper. Every once in a while, Sammie would gaze into space, then scribble with abandon. The pictures didn't make any sense to Carrie, who viewed them upside down and only in passing. Whenever Carrie neared, Sammie swiped the picture out of view.

"Aunt Carrie."

Carrie jumped, not having heard the girl approach. Not the best parenting tactic to let a child sneak up on someone holding a knife. She glanced down to where Sammie stood at her elbow. "Yes?"

"I finished my list of names for the kitten."

Carrie held her in surprise. Was that the mad scribbles the girl had been doing? Did she not know letters at all? "I have wet hands. Why don't you read them to me?"

Sammie nodded. "I thought up names for all three. The first one is Brownie, like I said before. 'Cause of the mom being Blackie."

"Okay." Carrie nodded. "What else?"

"Well, you said maybe not call him Brownie just because I thought of it right away. So I thought Sundae, like with ice cream."

Carrie laughed. "Were you hungry when you made the list?"

A giggling Sammie shook her head, the brown braids whipping her cheeks. "No, but I like sundaes and chocolate is brown like the kitty. I also thought maybe the shy one could be Peepers because she's always hiding and watching. Or Scatters, because that's what she does when you see her."

"Scatters? That's a big name." Was that a normal word for a five-year-old to know? Maybe Sammie's vocabulary was larger than she thought.

Of course, hearing adults say it didn't equal knowing how to spell it. Maybe Sammie had learned the phonetic, "sounding it out" strategy on the rodeo circuit. Something Ryan had taken the time to teach her? Not knowing frustrated Carrie. She reached for a towel and dried her hands. The carrots could wait. "May I see your list?"

Sammie slid back a step, eyes squeezing nearly closed as her face puckered like she'd eaten a lime. "You said I should read it to you 'cause I would know what it says."

"That's true, I did." *Darn it.*

"But I made some pictures you can see," the girl offered as though she were royalty bestowing leniency on a peasant.

"I'd love to."

Sammie climbed up on the chair and knelt, bouncing, her little mouth gone from lime-tart to dental-cleaning wide. "This is Scatters. I mean, if you want to call her that."

Carrie glanced at the blob of brown and white kitten then did a double take. There wasn't a figure, exactly, only colors that appeared as though they were moving. But darned if this didn't look like

Scatters had just been there and taken off, spooked by someone spotting her. If Carrie tried to draw a cat—or anything, she'd start with an outline then color inside the lines. The conventional way.

But she sure wouldn't have produced anything that resembled this.

Even more incredibly, above the blur, Sammie had indicated this to be SCATERS.

Pretty darn remarkable.

"I asked Daddy how to spell 'scat.' He says it all the time, so I figured he'd know how. Is that okay that he helped?"

Who does he say "scat" to, and how often is "all the time?" Carrie pushed the thought aside for later mulling. "That's fine. Your letters are" —beyond your age, amazingly well-formed, more legible than mine become late at night— "perfect."

Sammie beamed and rifled through the pile for another picture. Carrie couldn't tear her gaze from watching Scatters move-but-not-move, but she forced her attention to the next paper. And her jaw dropped.

"This is you and Daddy."

"I can see that. It's...fantastic."

A woman with a brown ponytail stood by a fence exactly like the corral outside her door. It could have been an artist's rendering for plans to build one, it was so detailed, down to the nails and hinges. She wore a red T-shirt, and an inch of bootheel showed under her jeans. On the other side of the fence, a man with Ryan's hair and smile sat atop a horse that resembled Cooper, including his socks and preferred bridle. Cooper smiled through the bit and had a tiny star drawn into his eye.

"Cooper doesn't really have a star in his eye even though I made him one. I saw one drawed like it in a book and wanted him to have a star too. Do you think Cooper would mind that it's not zactly like him?"

"No, he won't mind."

"'Cause I think he really does have a star, but we just can't see it all the time. It's probably there when he smiles."

"Well, he does smile," Carrie said.

Sammie nodded. "I've seen it."

The drawing showed no outline or erase marks Carrie could see. She'd titled it "DADDY AND ANT CARRIE."

"Who taught you to make letters?" When no answer came, Carrie turned away from the picture to see Sammie's face had closed. "Because he or she did a good job," Carrie rushed on. "You spell well and your letters are nicely made."

Sammie's face returned to its beam. "Letters are easy, once I know what ones to make. It's like drawing but you gotta do the straights and curves the way everyone else does. I make my letters like I see in books. I told you we go to the library in all the towns we visit. And Miss Callie, she's our teacher at rodeo, she teached me about letters and numbers. I can spell your name easy 'cause I learned how to spell hers and they're so much alike." She pointed, becoming a little chatterbox now. "See, you gotta change the L-L for R-R."

"Well, Miss Callie has done a tremendous job. Really amazing."

"Thanks."

"Do you have more pictures?"

"Sure!"

Carrie sank onto the chair beside Sammie, and for the next fifteen minutes oohed and aahed with genuine pleasure over the girl's art and letters.

Though she wrote all in capitals, the letters were perfectly formed, as though printed from a press. Carrie didn't think she could produce that steady and uniform a line, and certainly hadn't at five. She'd seen papers her mother had kept of all the kids' kindergarten days. She'd turned some of her letters backward, and nothing had been to scale. Her Rs had looked more like horses than her horse drawings.

What did that mean for Sammie? Was she a protégé? A budding genius? Did a scale of genius exist for forming letters? And what kind of career did that lead to? Carrie smiled at herself, a little breathless and getting carried away.

Because while the letters were impressive, the drawings were almost beyond belief. Sammie had drawn each kitten several times. Where more than one feline appeared, the distinctions made them recognizable. More amazing yet, each showed personality. Scatters never stood still, which sounded crazy as she thought it, admiring a two-dimensional crayon scribble. Blackie oversaw her offspring with maternal pride coupled with tolerance. Carrie could almost hear Blackie sigh in the picture of the third, as-yet-unnamed kitten being pounced on by Brownie/Sundae. Pouncing was a key life skill, so Blackie appeared both proud and resigned at their tussling. Seemed that little Nameless would be bullied unless he learned to pounce on his siblings during play. And it all came through in a child's drawing.

Would her friend Lexi's sister, Grace, be able to evaluate these simple-but-not-simple drawings? Grace had been considered a talented painter since her childhood. She'd encouraged Carrie's photography. Maybe she'd be willing to give her and Ryan some guidance on what to do with Sammie's abilities.

"Can I have some of these?"

Sammie nodded. "I can make more. And we gotta name the third one."

Pulled back to the mundane but eager to learn how Sammie's mind worked, Carrie asked, "What were you thinking?"

"Well, Daddy says he's a runt. That it won't turn out good for him if he's always..." She paused to think before adding, "Timid?"

Carrie nodded. "It means he's not brave."

"Daddy told me. So, I thought I'd call him Timmy. But I don't want to remind him when he's older that he used to be a scaredy cat." She laughed.

Carrie chuckled. "No. No one wants to be reminded of that."

"So I thought of what he'd be like when he's older. Brave, I hope." Sammie sorted through her papers for one near the bottom. Above the drawing of little Nameless she'd written BRAVO.

Carrie grinned. "I like it."

"Daddy really came up with it. I said I wanted the kitten to have a name he'd be proud of when he's older, and Daddy said, 'Bravo, Sammie.' He meant 'bravo' for the idea, but I like it for the kitty's name too."

Carrie gave her a hug. "It's settled then. Blackie's babies are Brownie, Scatters, and Bravo."

Sammie beamed so hard happy tears came to her eyes. Carrie soaked in the child's joy, trying to etch her face onto her heart for after they left. All she'd have were memories like this.

"Thank you, Aunt Carrie!" Sammie hugged Carrie's neck and held on tightly. The warm weight of the girl pressed against her brought tears to

Carrie's eyes. She didn't know how she'd bear the pain when Sammie and Ryan returned to the circuit.

~~~

Carrie watched the expressions flit across the face of her best friend's sister as Grace evaluated Sammie's drawings in the Moore kitchen. With her stomach churning like a backstage mom's, Carrie fought to keep quiet.

And lost. "Well, what do you think? Does she have talent?"

Grace nodded and Carrie about fainted with relief.

"But you knew that. You've got an artistic eye."

"I'm too close to Sammie."

"That's a topic for another day," Grace murmured. "What are you doing about your own photography? I've seen your postcards around town. And I know you're working for Kent. But are you pursuing something more? Are you at least submitting to magazines?"

"Not recently. I've been focused on the ranch."

"You can do both, you know."

Carrie gave a reluctant shrug of agreement. Photography was a hobby. The Moore Ranch was her passion. And yet, she seldom went anywhere without a camera. She viewed everything as though framing a shot. "I'll work on some submissions this weekend. I have a job that might yield some interesting shots."

"The wedding? Could be promising."

"Now that you've badgered me—and thank you, I suppose, for the encouragement, since you're the only person who ever asks about my photos—what about Sammie?"

"There's something there, as you saw. She has an unusual way of drawing, and of capturing more than the physical. Everyone can see those elements; a true artist can make you see what's not there. And I'd say Sam is extraordinary. Forget that she's five. This is amazing work for any age."

"Really?"

"The one of the cat that looks like it's moving?" Grace shook her head. "Extraordinary. And inspiring. Makes me itch to get to my easel."

"I knew it!" Carrie gave a short squeal then sobered slowly. "Crap. Right?"

Grace tilted her head in acknowledgment.

"What do I do with her now?"

"Do you mean nature or nurture?"

Carrie nodded.

"Well, that's a hard one for a parent." She shot Carrie a quick glance. "Or a family member advising a parent."

Carrie gave an acknowledging gesture. "Go on."

"She has innate talent, but it doesn't necessarily mean she can't improve. Talent needs to be practiced and polished. And, I believe, the right environment, instruction, and practice can help her grow into a truly exceptional talent."

Carrie slumped. Great news she didn't want to hear. "Ryan can't provide that for her while he's riding the circuit."

"Every artist's parent wants the child to have a normal life, right? The life, in this case, that has already brought forth such talent, since I'm guessing she's had no training."

"Right."

"But would a so-called normal life deny the artistic part of the girl? No one would watch a boy throw a football three hundred yards and do nothing."

Carrie bit back a smile. "Three hundred yards?"

"Shut up. Sports aren't my thing."

"Obviously."

"And you didn't call me here to talk sportsball."

"Point made."

"Some experts would say this talent needs to be nurtured. Send the girl to an art school. Perhaps in a year or two, a boarding school with a strong emphasis on the arts."

Carrie's eyes went wide. "Boarding school?"

"I know some I could recommend, even one in the States. Sam would graduate with stunning work, precise skills and technique. And this U.S. school is excellent at not boxing in an artist's natural talent."

Carrie shook her head. "Ryan will never go for it. I'm not sure it's what I'd want for Sammie either. Her going away."

"It would be hard, I know. But these past few years I spent traveling the world, rubbing elbows with other artists, perfecting my technique, experiencing life? If I'd had formal training, just think how much sooner I might have developed."

"You'd have been separated from your family. From Lexie."

Grace waved a hand in dismissal. "Twins are never really separated. Do you think drawing makes

Sam happy?"

"It's all she wants to do. But then, she's five. It's not like she's done a lot of other things. Ryan would never agree to sending her away, and I don't want her to go either."

"Sounds like your mind is made up."

Carrie nodded. "On boarding school, yes. We're against it. But what do we do for Sammie now?"

"Protect her in public school. Make sure you talk to her teachers. Don't let them tell Sam to color inside the lines. Show the teacher these drawings and watch how she reacts. If she thinks they're scribbles, don't let her near Sam. Home-school her if you have to."

Carrie groaned. "Ryan doesn't have much access to that being on the road."

Grace lifted a brow. "Then maybe Sam shouldn't be on the road."

CHAPTER SIX

Carrie met Matt at the diner two days later toward the end of her shift. A glorious morning out riding with the hands had renewed her energy and joy. She couldn't let her roping get rusty or let the herding dogs forget who was in charge. If she could bottle the scent of cattle under the sun, and of the land pushing up the smell of life in tufts of grass and clover and even weeds, then combine it with Cooper's skin radiating its own heated aroma, she'd make a wonderful perfume. Of course, only ranchers would want it, and they had access to it all naturally. She smiled at her idiocy. There went that million-dollar idea.

She'd given the question of Sammie's education some of that energy and come up with several solutions. Hopefully running it past a third party would help her reach a decision.

"It sounds like you've already decided," Matt said as she finished laying out the variables while he finished his late dinner. He set his cutlery on the plate and wiped his mouth with a napkin. Even though he was a laid-back cowboy with slow mannerisms, these were stalling tactics for sure.

She frowned. "I haven't decided anything. That's the problem. There are too many things to consider."

"Like the girl's father." His hard tone surprised her.

"Of course I'm thinking of Ryan too. He's not going to want to grant me custody of Sammie."

Matt's brows lowered. "Custody? Don't you mean guardianship, as in, it being a short-term deal?"

"Whatever it's called. I don't know how long Ryan will be on the rodeo circuit. I should have legal authority to make decisions for Sammie."

"Hasn't he been doing a good job raising her so far?" Matt leaned back and crossed his arms over his chest. "Or don't you think a single father can raise a child properly?"

"Whoa." Carrie drew back. "Where'd that come

from?" She caught movement in her peripheral vision and hoped no one would come talk to them right now. When she saw it was the young woman who came into the diner every few days, she waved a hand in greeting as the new arrival passed on the way to the restroom.

Glancing around, she noticed other customers averting their gazes. The discussion with Matt had drawn unwanted attention. She made an effort to keep her voice low. "I never said anything about single dads in general or that Ryan was a bad father."

"Then why take his kid from him? Because Grace said she can draw?"

"And for all the reasons I told you." She ticked each on a finger as she listed them. "Schooling being number one. Bullying by those boys she mentioned. The ladies Ryan has been spending time with, as far as being a temporary distraction for him and an influence on her. The danger of his job. Not to mention, who watches her when he's practicing and competing? And, with the very real possibility of another bad fall, what happens to Sammie before Adam and I can get to her? How long before we even learn of his accident...or something worse?"

His jaw set. "Sounds like things Winslow should deal with. Maybe he already has plans in place. Have you talked to him?"

"No."

"Do you have any proof he's been a bad father?"

"Of course not."

"Yet you'd take his child from him."

"Stop saying it like that."

Matt reached across the table and took her hand. "It *is* like that, Carrie. And that's what bothers you."

She grimaced at him and ignored his responding smile. "Stop acting like you can read my mind."

"But I can. You have a kind heart. I'd be surprised if all this didn't bother you. And yet you persevere because of that kind heart."

"Catch-22? I do what I do because of my so-called kind heart, yet that same heart makes me regret what I do. Doesn't seem fair."

"Ask Winslow who watches Sammie while he's riding and practicing. Maybe he has a regular babysitter the girl is comfortable with. Ask him what the plans are if he's injured. Make sure you're first on the call list and everyone knows your number."

She scowled. "Those are good ideas."

Matt suppressed a smile but not before she saw it. "Honey, I believe a man can be as good a single parent as a woman can. Agree?"

She nodded.

"So, bring your concerns to Winslow. If he can fix them, he will."

"He can't fix the main problem, Matt." She pulled her hand away to wipe at the table with a napkin. "He's got to stay on the rodeo circuit. Which is not only a questionable environment for a child, but she also spends so much time alone. She should be in school this year, and not only for her art development—and I see you trying not to roll your eyes at that—but for socialization."

"Art is important in the world," Matt said solemnly.

"Don't humor me."

"I'm not. It is important. I'm just not sure I agree that art *school* is important for a five-year-old. Sammie has developed so far on her own. Maybe that's what she needs to continue doing."

"Are you saying that to make me stop talking about keeping her?"

"No, but I'm on Winslow's side on this, honey. I'm sorry. I don't think it's fair to take his child from him."

Carrie dropped her gaze to the table. "I didn't say it's fair to Ryan. But is it fair to Sammie *not* to bring her into our home?"

"Okay, if you have concerns, take the kid to the doctor. See if she's healthy, at normal weights and heights and all that."

"That's exactly the problem. I don't have the legal right to even get her any type of health care."

"Okay, so have Winslow sign off on you taking her to the appointment while he's busy at Windy Glade. You can get the outcome from the doc while you're there. Girl's gotta have a physical before kindergarten, right? Even if she doesn't stay here for school, this ticks a box. Gives him options."

"That's a good idea. I'll see if I can swing it."

"If not, at least ask to go with him when he takes her. He shouldn't have a reason to object."

"Okay." She nodded with excitement. "Okay. I see a plan coming together."

~~~

Not only did Ryan not object to her going with them to the doctor, he made sure she could listen to the doctor's report in his office. Sammie remained a little underweight for her age, but given she also stood taller than the normal percentile, the doc was satisfied with her progress. Hearing, sight, et cetera all checked out. At Carrie's suggestion, Sammie received the inoculations she needed to attend kindergarten. Just in case.

Having the child between them in the truck cab kept the ride from being awkward. Sammie chattered away as Ryan sped back to drop off Carrie. They'd both stolen time from their ranches.

After her afternoon shift at Leo's, Carrie took a pie over to Ryan as a thank you for his including her. She peeked in the front screen door to see if Sammie was awake. What she saw made her brow furrow: Ryan wincing and rubbing his shoulder as he cleaned up the kitchen.

She gave a light tap at the door before entering. He didn't smile when he looked up and saw her, so she extended the pie plate. That did change his expression. At least he perked up on seeing the pie.

"A thank you," she said.

"For?"

"For you letting me go with you to the appointment. I know you didn't have to, and I appreciate it."

"What kind?"

She arched a brow at him. "Does it matter?"

He did grin at her then before turning to retrieve three plates.

Three. She hid her pleasure. If he could be stoic, she could at least try to be. "Is she still awake?"

"In the tub."

"By herself?"

His face went blank, meaning he heard her censure. "I'm listening for splashing. Since she takes that toy horse into the tub with her, she talks to him the whole time."

"Sorry if that sounded..." Carrie couldn't think of a word.

"As though I don't take care of Sammie?"

She winced but nodded.

"It's okay. You can bring another pie tomorrow to make up for it."

She smiled in relief.

They ate the Dutch apple pie as Sammie regaled

them with a tale about Charming's adventures in the bathtub. Afterward, the adults took turns reading Sammie a story each and kissing her goodnight.

"I like this," Sammie said to Ryan as he tucked the sheet under her chin. "I wish I got two stories every night."

"Then it wouldn't be a treat." But he heard the longing in her voice. Loneliness? Need for a mother figure?

Trudging downstairs, he considered his own loneliness and need. No one could replace Hannah, but he could see maybe making room for another person in their lives. A person Sammie would love, but who wouldn't expect the enthusiasm of first love from him. He'd have to find the *right* person, which, given he had so much to do around Windy Glade, after competing to earn sufficient prize money, didn't seem likely any time soon.

"I noticed you stopped wearing your sling," Carrie said.

Ryan nodded. "Can't get the work done otherwise. I have some prescription cream for when it hurts bad."

"Do you need help rubbing it on your back?"

When he stared, she shrugged. "I saw you through the door. Looked like you probably can't reach. Call it an extension of the thank you visit. Same as I'd do for Adam." When she hesitated, she added, "Or Cooper."

Mention of her horse made him chuckle. Tempted to refuse just on principle, he weighed the benefit of less pain against his pride. Maybe he'd sleep better using the medicated ointment, which he had to admit, he hadn't been able to apply himself. "Thanks."

He unbuttoned his shirt in the bathroom where Carrie wouldn't see the slow movements of his pain, then brought the cream into the living room. He studied the couch, pictured her behind him rubbing his body. Yanking a wooden chair from the table, he straddled it with his arms on the top rail. Raising his arms that high made him grit his teeth, but at least he didn't moan.

Carrie squirted ointment on her hands then whisked them together. He appreciated not having the cold cream touch his back.

"Where's it hurt?"

Ryan couldn't say "everywhere," so he

described the worst spot. She didn't hesitate in smoothing the medicine on. He could picture her doing the same for her brother—or her horse—and he relaxed into the sensation. The cream started warm then turned cold, and his body shivered. The pressure increased as she began rubbing, using the heel of her hands to knead his pain away.

He moaned, then, embarrassed, said, "Sorry."

"For?" She echoed his earlier question about her apology pie.

Ryan smiled as his tension eased.

"Better, or am I pressing too hard? Or in the wrong spot?"

He shook his head then let it hang so she could reach his neck area. "Everything feels great."

Carrie rubbed his neck, decreasing her pressure along the sensitive nerve. She moved her hands to his non-sore shoulder, and he realized "non-sore" didn't apply. He moaned involuntarily again but didn't apologize.

"You've been overworking this side to save strain on the injured side."

"You're good at this."

"I've had plenty of practice. Dad had that bad

knee. Mom had arthritis in her shoulder. Adam has gotten plenty of aches working the ranch."

Ryan tried to turn to see her and she paused, leaning toward him. "And you? Who tends your aches?"

The words pulsed in the air, raising the tension as they hung with an intended meaning. Their gazes locked. He imagined hands, his hands, on her naked back, rubbing, smoothing, caressing.

He swallowed hard past a jolt of desire. "That didn't come out right."

His voice was thick. He saw her brown eyes had darkened and he almost sagged with relief. At least she felt something too. If this had become a stupid moment, they were both participating.

She didn't move away, suspended over his shoulder as though a puppet awaiting a tug on her strings. Her mouth opened then closed. She cleared her throat but no words came.

They stared into each other's eyes. They both breathed hard. Silence pounded between them. Or maybe his heart had just throbbed back to life, fluttering like a baby bird escaping its shell, both protection and cage. Before he could wrap his mind around this astonishing feeling, she straightened and removed her hands.

"I should go."

~~~

Carrie took an extra shift at the diner the next day, her mind in a turmoil and needing something to do. Ranch work had worn off some of her edginess that morning, but not all. Having those kinds of feelings for Ryan confused her. Not only was he her sister's husband, but she had Matt to consider. She shouldn't be experiencing any awareness of Ryan's masculinity. But her hands tingled whenever she recalled the rubdown she'd given him and the way it ended. The heat of his muscles beneath her hands. The urge to smooth and kiss away his pain. When he'd emerged from the hall with the liniment and she'd seen him without his shirt, she shouldn't have reacted at all. Another cowboy, another chest. She'd seen them all her life.

Granted, he had a nice muscular chest, tanned and taut, with exactly the right amount of hair. She'd never considered whether she liked hair on a man's chest, but on Ryan—

But she couldn't think that way. He'd been

Hannah's husband. He loved her sister. Always had, always would. And even if he didn't, if he could make room in his heart for another woman, that woman shouldn't be her.

Carrie couldn't imagine who would be right for him. Just not herself.

When her best friend, Lexi, walked in with her stepdaughter, Anna, in the early afternoon, Carrie had to resist the urge to pull her friend aside for some advice. Lexi had married a widower, and he'd been set to marry Lexi's twin sister, Grace, to boot. Lexi had had to overcome two women in his heart. She'd be the voice of experience Carrie needed. Given eight-year-old Anna's presence, though, any woman talk would have to wait.

They waved and took seats in a booth. As the only waitress working, every section was Carrie's, so she went over for their order.

"What are you doing here?" Lexi asked.

Avoiding Ryan. "Took an extra shift."

"Where's Beatrice?"

"Johnny's leg is acting up."

Lexi grimaced. Johnny had lost his leg in Nam half a century before. It "acting up" meant either he had crazy-bad pain in his body or PTSD. His wife waitressed at the diner as much for socializing as the paycheck. And Carrie had to hand it to Leo, Beatrice's paycheck had extra padding some weeks. Customers left what tips they could, giving help in a way Beatrice could accept, in a way Johnny could accept. Often, part of a slaughtered cow would be left off at the kitchen for Beatrice to take home. Hunters took meat to Johnny directly, their own freezers "too full." Carrie didn't want to live anywhere but Little Tree for reasons like those. These neighbors cared and showed it, and usually in a way that showed respect for Johnny and Beatrice.

"She's coming in tonight, after his meds ease him." Carrie changed the subject. "How's Jack's brother?"

"He came home for Anna's birthday, but he had something or *someone* on his mind. I'm sure we'll find out soon."

"Mom brought me in for ice cream," Anna piped up.

"A girls' outing," Lexi said.

Carrie smiled. "Happy belated birthday. Should I see what kind of cake or pie we might have in the kitchen to go with it?"

"Yes, please."

"For me too," Lexi said. "Dad's in the office so I'm on call, but Anna likes to come along if the situation isn't dangerous." Lexi referred to her work as a veterinarian.

"Lucky you."

And they were lucky, Carrie thought, as Anna decided on the flavor of her sundae. Anna's mother had passed from a fall off a horse when the girl was a toddler. Her dad, Jack, had done well by her—another widowed father who made raising a daughter seem easy, and Lexi had completed the family unit with her marriage to him a few months prior. She and Anna had forged a tight bond Carrie envied.

Might she and Sammie have that kind of relationship someday? If Ryan let Carrie raise her until he finished with rodeo, in a few months or years, or however long it took, would Sammie come to think of Carrie as a substitute mother? Closer than an aunt or a friend. Carrie already loved the girl with what she supposed were a mother's feelings. The same she'd seen in Lexi toward Anna. Could she have that too?

Taking their treats to their table, Carrie nodded a hello toward the girl with the backpack who came in every day or so. Maybe when Carrie wasn't on shift as well, for all she knew. The girl came in between meals, during hours when it wasn't crowded, like the time when Carrie brought her eggs, and she'd left the dollar tip for a free meal.

Carrie thought of her as "the camper" because after she used the restroom, she came out looking fresher, and usually in a different shirt. Where the girl camped, Carrie didn't know. Some ranchers gave permission for an overnight stay. Though now that Carrie thought about it, the twenty-ish girl had been coming in for almost a week. Maybe she needed the solitude, as an artist or writer, and had struck up an agreement to camp. That was Little Tree for you. Hospitality to the core.

"Be right with you," Carrie called.

The girl nodded and kept walking.

"Who's that?" Lexi asked, watching the girl's back.

"A new regular. Not sure."

"Find out?"

"Didn't want to pry. But yeah. It's time to welcome her to town."

Shorthand for making sure the girl was okay. Women taking care of women.

"No scuff marks," Carrie continued, mindful of Anna. "But thin. Alone."

"Let me pay for her food today," Lexi said. "That welcome to town."

Their gazes met and the women silently communicated their concern, a benefit of having been friends since childhood.

"Everything okay with you?" Carrie asked, with a slight head jerk toward Anna.

Lexi's smile beamed. "Better than okay on all fronts."

Carrie squeezed a hug onto her friend's shoulder before moving to the other customer's table. Afternoons were slow, which gave her time to work in the office on the paperwork Leo hated. He could tend to it himself and had for years. He merely preferred to review the work Carrie did and sign off on her numbers rather than generating the reports himself. He gave Carrie a little extra for "saving his eyesight," which she gratefully accepted. Leo also preferred his kitchen to people or office work. They made a good team since Carrie didn't mind any of it.

"Hi," she said as she approached the girl with a full glass of ice water with a lemon slice on the side. "How are you today?"

"Good, thanks. And you?" She had a quiet voice and Carrie estimated she was about twenty years old. Her golden-brown hair hung damply past her shoulders and Carrie suspected she'd washed it in the bathroom sink again. She wore a pink T-shirt now as opposed to the dark blue she'd worn when she entered. Carrie guessed wherever she camped didn't offer running water.

"Doing well, thanks," she replied. "I noticed you've been coming in every few days now."

The girl tensed.

"And I feel bad I haven't greeted you properly," Carrie continued. "I'm Carrie Moore. Welcome to Little Tree."

The girl wiped her hand on her thigh. Why would she be nervous about introducing herself? Maybe she was just that shy.

"Brandi."

Carrie opened her mouth instinctively, then

closed it. Brandi didn't care to add her last name. Had her parents taught her to be careful with information, or was she protecting her identity?

The girl grinned, her light brown eyes glowing, and her face turning almost luminescent. "I know. I'm a *fine girl*."

Carrie laughed as the girl quoted the song that now popped into Carrie's head. "I bet you get that a lot."

"I don't mind. It's my dad's favorite."

"Did he serve in the Navy?"

Brandi shook her head. "Mom teases him that he just likes the idea. A love so true the woman is unable to get over a man, even though he won't commit. She says Dad's a romantic."

Carrie relaxed, glad to hear the girl talk about her parents in a positive way. So probably not a runaway. But she struck Carrie as fragile, which was why she thought of "the camper" as "the girl," not "the woman."

"I always thought of that Brandy as a tragic figure," Carrie said, "but she has her love for this guy, I guess."

Brandi shrugged. "He always comes back to her.

That's all the love he has to offer, and he gives it to her. According to Dad, you can't change a person or ask them to be something they're not."

"I guess."

The girl slanted her a look with shining eyes and a smile playing around her lips. "And, of course, a man probably wrote it."

Carrie laughed. "Of course."

After a moment, Carrie asked, "What can I get you today? We have a meatloaf special. Comes with garlic mashed potatoes, vegetables and a drink." Thinking of Lexi and Anna, Carrie tacked on, "And dessert of your choice."

When Brandi hesitated, Carrie went on. "No fish today, sorry. But everything else on the menu comes with your choice of a starch, vegetables, a drink, and dessert."

Since Lexi would leave money for the meal, Carrie didn't mind the white lie. She could make up any extra costs.

"Wow, that's a lot of food."

In Carrie's opinion, the girl could use a lot of food. Hollows darkened her cheeks, and the light bruising under her eyes—from too little sleep Carrie guessed—tinged her smooth, pale skin. "I recommend the special if you like meatloaf. Leo makes the best outside of my mom's kitchen. All the food groups represented if you add milk to the meal."

Brandi took a deep breath and blew it out softly. "That sounds healthy. I'll try it please. With milk."

"Free refills on the milk, of course." Carrie swished away before her ears burned red. She hadn't lied. Milk came with free refills, but she worried she'd manipulated Brandi into ordering more food than the girl felt she could pay for. Brandi didn't know the meal would be free and Carrie had put her in a tough position. Brandi usually ordered milk and the special, occasionally the four-dollar breakfast, which they served all day. Carrie wondered what else Brandi ate.

Later, when Brandi asked for the bill, Carrie dreaded the exchange. "You're paid for. Not by me. Some other customers who haven't met you yet."

"The woman and little girl?" Brandi asked. "They waved to me."

"They couldn't stay to greet you properly and felt bad for not doing so. Came and went." Carrie shrugged, as though this was no big thing.

Brandi glanced around the now empty room, a little frantic, a little alarmed. "But... I can pay."

"Not today. It's taken care of."

"But... why? I don't know anyone here, except you."

Carrie didn't ask why that was. "It's Little Tree hospitality. Sometime in the future, you can pay for someone else's meal. It's not a big deal. Is it?"

"I guess not. But I don't want to be a charity case."

"It's hospitality."

"But..." The girl frowned, looking doubtful. Although there were probably only a handful of years between Brandi and Carrie's own twenty-seven, the girl's vulnerability made her seem younger.

Carrie sat in the seat opposite. "You're a regular customer now, Brandi. You've paid in the past. This is just a 'howdy.' No one thinks of it as charity."

"How do you know you're not being taken advantage of? That someone wouldn't merely freeload?"

"My job on earth is to be kind and helpful. The Lord can sort out who's deserving and who's taking advantage." When Brandi didn't appear convinced,

Carrie added, "God loves a cheerful giver."

"That's from the Bible."

"It's hard to be on the receiving end. I've been there. So now I give."

"Pay it forward?"

"Just a 'howdy,'" Carrie repeated.

Brandi blew out a breath. "When you see that woman and girl again, tell them thanks. And howdy back."

Carrie smiled as she rose. "Welcome to Little Tree."

CHAPTER SEVEN

On Saturday, Carrie took pictures of the happy couple, liking the lovely cream satin gown of the bride, edging toward blush, a subtle tone she herself could imagine wearing that photographed beautifully. About a third of the small town had attended, keeping with the couple's modest budget. Culling the list must have been hard, Carrie thought as she snapped another photo, this one of the flower girl and ring bearer—the ranch dog that kept herding the girl where it wanted her to go. When the bride and groom knew everyone in town, and their parents had friends and obligatory invites, *and* the bridal couple had made friends at college, the number of potential guests no doubt rivaled that of Santa's "naughty or nice" list.

She smirked as she considered telling Matt he'd landed on the naughty list. He understood budgeting and hadn't known the couple all that well, so he hadn't been bothered about not attending, other than it separating them for the evening.

The expressions on the couple's faces caught Carrie's attention more than the trimmings and frills. She hoped she captured their joyful, awed look of love that said "why didn't we do this sooner" mixed with a tinge of "why didn't we just elope?" Carrie had to remind herself to photograph not only the wedding couple but the cake, the family, and the dancing, and make sure she had everyone present recorded. She took generic pictures of decorations for stock photo websites. Additional income, wherever it may come from.

Yet through all that, she remained ever-conscious of Ryan's whereabouts. It bothered her to be so aware of him. Of his tall, fit figure. Of her reaction to how he looked in a suit, which was basically to get him alone and out of that suit. A disturbing thought. While she acknowledged her physical attraction to him, she couldn't lie to herself that his allure stopped there. She noticed his smile, the attention he paid to everyone. He did a tame version of the twist with the flower girl, keeping his arms close to his sides. She noticed him compensating for his injury but doubted others did. He executed a nifty foxtrot with the groom's grandmother, who had also been his third-grade teacher. Later, he became noticeably absent when the groom tossed the garter for his bachelor friends. Or at least, noticeably to her.

They'd matched glances a few times, shared smiles across the church then at the reception. The groom's family had set up an area on their ranch, with a canopy sheltering a bar and eating area, and a temporary dance floor specially constructed for the evening.

Her hyper-awareness of Ryan prepared her for his appearance at her side later into the evening when the dancing had surpassed its peak. At least, she hoped the party would wind down. Morning loomed and her feet hurt from wearing even her sensible heels.

"Have you had any food yet?" he asked.

"I always eat beforehand, and I snuck a bite while Kent took pictures." She shot him a smile.

"Who can resist cake?"

"Got a piece to put under your pillow?"

She arched her eyebrows. "To dream about my future husband? No."

"Sammie asked me to bring her a piece."

"What did you say?"

"I told her it was too messy and she's too young anyway."

Carrie held his gaze.

He tilted his head and shrugged. "It's in a napkin in my coat pocket."

A place in her heart melted. "Softie."

He gave a *what can you do* gesture. "Can you take a break and dance?"

Startled, Carrie glanced at him, then at the remaining people.

"The bride and groom have left the building, so to speak."

She nodded. "I know. I have some great shots of them leaving. Someone instructed the dog to herd them into the car, which got on video. It's about time to wrap it up."

"Which means you do have a minute."

She ducked her head in a reluctant nod.

"Dance with me."

Simple. Direct. Friendly.

So why did her heart pound crazily?

He was her brother-in-law, for Pete's sakes. He'd be embarrassed if he knew of her reaction. *She'd* be embarrassed if he knew. She took an extra minute to secure her cameras from being knocked to the ground or "borrowed." It always amazed her how many people thought it would be okay to shoot a picture with her unattended equipment. Because they had a camera somewhat like it. Or they were too drunk to use common sense. Or sometimes a child couldn't resist touching.

But her camera was an essential part of her work. It didn't pay one-third of her bills, despite being part of her third job, aside from waitressing and the ranch. Photography didn't put bread on the table, exactly, but it provided the ice cream, bailed Adam out of the drunk tank, and once, the income had enabled her to go to Billings with friends to see a musical and stay overnight. Plus, she enjoyed the challenge of taking the perfect shot, setting the exposure, getting the angle, capturing the expression or the animal or the sunset at exactly the right time, with just the right light. Developing her photos was both expensive and totally worth it. Just not always monetarily.

"I like that color on you," Ryan said as they took to the dance floor. He ran his hand down her periwinkle dress, stopping at her waist. It felt almost casual and almost a caress.

She fought to ignore that last idea. "I'm supposed to be invisible."

He drew away to glance at her, a question on his face.

"I'm a worker, not a guest." She shrugged. "People either tense up around cameras or ham it up. It's better if no one notices me."

"Do you really think that's possible?"

The deepened tone of his voice gave the remark more importance than the words carried. His intent gaze made her suppress a tremble.

Before she could think of a response, he pulled her closer and rested his chin near her temple. He tucked his left elbow close to his side, protecting his injured shoulder, and settled both hands at her waist. She fought a shiver of awareness as she set her hands on his shoulders.

"Everyone sees you, Carrie," he said in a near-whisper into her hair. "No matter how you try to hide."

She shrugged, uncomfortable with his closeness and his tenderness, both in touch and tone. "That's sweet but—"

"Let's just dance," he interrupted her softly. "Let's simply be a woman and a man, under the night sky and the party lights."

She shouldn't be aware of him, not as a woman to a man. It would be awkward at best. She feared driving a wedge between them that might make his visits to Little Tree even less frequent.

Since he asked, she tried...and found it easier than she'd have imagined. They fit together dancing, their steps aligning, their bodies moving together without thought. Her mom had taught all four of them, after all, so his moves were familiar, though she'd learned by dancing with a reluctant Adam.

Ryan's muscled strength lured her in, tempting her to snuggle against him. He smelled of the outdoors, fresh wind, and the beer he'd had earlier. The warmth of the sun lingered on his skin while the night air whispered through his hair. She yearned to stroke a few strands into place, to trail her fingers down his now-scruffy cheek.

Dammit. She fisted her hands on his shoulders and stood straight. Peeking around the dance area that had been constructed, it surprised her the crowd's eyes weren't drilling into them as she'd feared. Maybe she really was invisible.

"No one's watching me now," she said, trying to lighten the mood. "Once the camera's gone, they forget why I'm here. I blend into the crowd. Good to know." She drew back and smiled, making the movement more natural, as though she only wanted to look into his face and share the joke, but not that she needed to back away for any other reason. "Maybe no one will notice when I go for that second piece of wedding cake from Frank's Bakery."

Ryan shook his head. "Them being used to you as a fixture in the town isn't quite the same as them not seeing you. We all see you. We see you running the ranch, working at the diner, helping out Lou, and taking extra shifts for Beatrice when her husband is experiencing one of his bouts with PTSD."

"That's tragic. I feel so bad for her. And Johnny."

"And you taking extra shifts helps her keep her

job."

"No," she protested. "That's all Lou. He keeps her job for her."

"You help him do that by not putting a burden on him."

She smirked. "Lou is perfectly capable of cooking, waiting tables, and busing them. He just doesn't like to deal with people."

"And you make that easier on him. He can continue his preferred role, keep his business running, and his clients happy because of you."

"You're making that a bigger deal than it is. I do get paid, you know."

"And you need that money. To keep Moore Ranch going. And to bail Adam out of jail."

She stiffened.

"Don't worry, that's all I'm saying about Adam and his drinking. It's too beautiful a night to argue about him."

"Plus, he's at home watching your child so you can talk up the ranchers here. How did that go?"

"Good. Gave me a lot to consider."

Silence settled between them as the soft music wrapped around them. The slow dance indicated the band planned to wrap it up for the evening, or so Carrie desperately hoped. The dark night, being held in Ryan's arms, his breath stirring her hair, his warmth enveloping her body— She shouldn't be stirred by him, not physically. It was bad enough she kept remembering that cake in his pocket, proving his love for his daughter, proving what a good man he was. The memory of him dancing with the grandma and the flower girl filled her heart. All his kindnesses moved her dangerously close to ... attraction. There she'd admitted it.

Ryan tilted his head. "Look at that moon."

Carrie worried if she tilted her head upwards, she'd grow light-headed. The joy of the wedding, the man before her, the intimacy of the night, her job complete and her responsibilities shed—all of it combined to sweep her into giddiness.

Of course, she couldn't cast off her responsibilities. Adam had stayed home with Sammie, so he wasn't out drinking, but... Adam had stayed home with Sammie. Despite her urging Ryan to give Adam a chance at being an uncle, at being responsible, she couldn't quite shove away her worry. She knew in her heart he wouldn't drink, not while babysitting. But choosing not to drink versus being barred from alcohol by responsibilities agitated different demons. She worried what resisting the siren call of alcohol would cost him in the coming days.

Ryan's hand appeared in line of sight right before his finger touched her between her brows. He rubbed a circle there. "It's too peaceful a night to be thinking deep thoughts."

"You mean I'm getting a wrinkle. That doesn't make me feel peaceful."

"Wrinkles don't matter on a face as full of character as yours."

Surprise pushed a laugh out of her. "Thanks?"

"And you're pretty anyway," Ryan continued. "But you know that."

"I'm not sure how to take that, any of that. Is it a compliment of some kind or a backhanded insult?"

"Just a statement of facts, ma'am."

"Hmm."

They danced quietly for a few steps. "I was thinking about Sammie. Wondering if she's asleep already and how she and Adam got along. Not worried," she added quickly. "I wouldn't have suggested Adam babysit if I had any doubt he could do it."

"Do it sober, you mean."

"Yes."

"Hopefully, he can hold out one night."

Carrie nodded. "It's tomorrow I worry about. The responsibility tonight might be too much for him. The pressure to not drink."

Ryan kissed her temple. She peered at him in surprise.

"Let tomorrow worry about tomorrow. It's coming anyway, no matter how much you fret. Take tonight for yourself. That's what I'm doing."

"What do you mean?"

"Tonight, I'm not a rodeo rider or a father or a widower or even a Winslow. I'm not a rancher or a horse tamer. Tonight, I'm simply being. I'm dancing with a pretty woman I'm very fond of. I'm enjoying the soft night and the ease of being with you."

"*Easy* meaning you don't have to impress me."

"I doubt if I could. We're comfortable together. And that feels pretty damn awesome right now. So, for a few more minutes, let's just dance."

~~~

"Uncle Adam" found her crayons and paper. Uncle Adam served dinner. Uncle Adam read her stories.

Uncle Adam didn't think about a stiff whiskey every single second.

That was what he told himself anyway. He wanted to make a connection with Sammie, but what did he know about kids? Even though he considered himself a decent older brother, he hadn't paid much attention to Carrie's everyday interests. She'd been easy to be around. She liked the same things he liked: horses and ranching. She and Hannah had neither one been into girl stuff, at least not that he'd noticed.

Another half hour passed. Uncle Adam needed to stop checking the clock so often. He couldn't will the hands to move faster.

"Can I have more lemonade, Uncle Adam?"

He smiled and served it, definitely not thinking about the mixers that could go in it to make it taste a thousand times better.

"Will you play a different game with me, Uncle Adam? That Operation guy's nose didn't go off, and I know you touched the sides a lot."

His dexterity might have suffered lately. Did they

have any other board games left in the house that a kid her age could play? "You know any card games?"

His adorable niece nodded, her brown eyes like every Moores' he'd ever seen. Something stirred inside him as he thought of his older sister and his parents. He owed it to them to straighten up and fly right.

At least for tonight.

He could sweat out this babysitting thing for another few hours. She had to go to sleep sometime, right?

Of course, then he'd have to stay alert in case she needed something in the night. Kids got thirsty. A tall cold glass of...

Nope. Wouldn't think about that. He tried to turn the haunting golden image into lemonade, but the foamy head wouldn't shrink. Bubbles rose up the side of the glass, which glistened with condensation. He swallowed. Go away, barley; go away, hops.

He shot a glance at the wall clock. How much longer till Carrie got home?

Adam made numerous trips to the bathroom to run water over his face and give his reflection a stern talking-to. "You can do this. It's only a few hours."

He hadn't had so much as a sip of alcohol in two hundred and seventeen days. Some easy days, some not so much. This was a "not so much" day. Being responsible for his niece underscored the impossibility of having a sip tonight, which he might not otherwise have even considered. Drink was more on his mind because he had to guard himself against the temptation. Shouldn't be a problem, he kept telling himself. *You didn't drink yesterday; you're not going to drink tomorrow. You should be able to get through tonight. You should be stronger than this.*

"Bedtime," he said with relief when they'd watched some cute video she'd sung along to. He couldn't name the movie with a gun to his head.

Sammie was old enough to get herself arranged for bed, which he considered a blessing. She'd brought pajamas to stay overnight, sleeping in his sisters' old room. She arranged all her stuff how she liked it and looked at him.

What did she expect now? He'd been three seconds from his getaway, but he couldn't budge until he'd finished his duty for the night.

He hovered in the doorway. "You got everything?"

She nodded, eyes big. "Thank you for keeping me tonight."

"Sure thing. You good?"

Despite her nod, he felt reluctant to leave her. Her gaze stayed glued to his face like a lifeline. He hated to tell her, but he couldn't be anyone's lifeline. Even his own. "Am I supposed to tell you a story or something?"

"I'd like that, but you don't have to. Daddy doesn't always."

"Okay then."

"But—" She shot upright. "Don't close the door all the way, okay?"

"No, no, of course not."

Sammie scooted down under the sheet, shifting some plastic toy by her. She gave him a hopeful smile. "Sometimes Aunt Carrie sings to me."

"Yeah, I don't think so."

"She does."

"My singing would give you nightmares." He doubted he knew any songs fit for young ears. Maybe he could play her one on his cell phone.

"That's okay." She gave a dramatic sigh. "I kinda wanted you to stay longer. For Charming. He's afraid of the dark sometimes."

Adam felt pretty sure he was being played. Songs and stories and staying longer. What was the kid up to? Nevertheless, he asked, "Charming?"

"My horse." She held up the plastic toy.

"Ah. Well." Chagrined, Adam came in and peered at the toy. "He's afraid, huh? Can I sit here or would he be upset?"

Sammie's mouth shifted side to side as she considered. "He'd like that. But don't pet him yet."

"Of course not. Some horses are skittish." Adam perched on the side of the mattress facing her, trying not to let his nerves show. "Even if you spend all day feeding them and playing games, they can be reluctant to bed down in a new stall."

"It isn't me, Uncle Adam," the girl said in exasperation. "I had fun tonight."

"Okay."

"It's Charming. He…" Sammie's fingers ran over the horse's dark mane. "He has nightmares sometimes. He's worried he'll get lost or left behind."

Her words punched into Adam's chest. And to his shame, he'd never wanted a drink more in his life.

"Well, uh, maybe Charming needs to be reminded that people, uh, that you love him and would never let that happen."

She nodded. "I tell him, but he's heard about it on the rodeo circuit. It happens, Uncle Adam. It happened to someone he knows."

"Here's the deal, though. There's always someone to take care of lost … horses. His friend it happened to—" Sweat broke out on his body. God, he was fumbling through this. *Give me a hint, Hannah.* He considered the horse and her fingers that had turned white holding the toy so tightly. "Look, Sammie, I'm gonna level with you. Sometimes bad things happen. You're old enough to know that. Hell, you've lived through it."

"You shouldn't swear."

"Did I? Oh, right. Sorry. I'm only saying, you lost your mom. My sister. And we both miss her."

He paused, waiting for inspiration. Sammie's intent gaze put him on the spot. He needed to say something reassuring.

"But your dad loves you and wouldn't let anything happen to you. And you've got Aunt Carrie who loves you and would turn cartwheels to make you happy."

She blinked. Waiting.

"And..." He took a deep breath. "You've got me."

After a pause while he tried to think what promises he could offer, she said, "Would you turn cartwheels for me?"

He snorted. "That'd be the day. Can you imagine? I'd probably break my nose falling on my face."

Sammie's laugh eased the pain in his chest.

"But I love you too, Sammie." He wanted to promise to be there for her. He knew better. "I'm pretty tough, and I can be mean when I need to. I won't let anything bad happen as long as I'm around."

He only hoped that was true.

She placed her small hand over his rough one. He sat still, overcome by her belief in him. "Charming feels better now."

"I'm glad." Adam could barely choke out the words, his throat had gone so dry. Maybe one glass wouldn't hurt. Okay, he wouldn't have a whole glass. Carrie hid a bottle of white wine in the back of the drawer of kitchen towels and potholders. Wine couldn't hurt anything. It hardly even counted as alco—

"Sometimes," Sammie said in a whisper he had to strain to hear, "Daddy sleeps on the floor by us. Would you do that tonight?"

Adam nodded. Laying at his niece's bedside would remind him of all the reasons he couldn't sneak downstairs for just a sip. *Just a sip* didn't exist in his world.

The trust in her smile broke his heart as he made sure she and the horse had sheets pulled over them. He couldn't believe he'd planned to go down and seek relief in a bottle of wine he wouldn't even get drunk on. Relief from what? Playing with a kid? Jesus. This kid needed him sober. Surely he could hang on for another few hours. Her request for him to sleep at her bedside had saved him from temptation. Well, no, drinking still tempted him. Her request had saved him from acting on temptation, at least for another night. He kissed the forehead of his little savior.

The hard floor was as good as he deserved.

~~~

Is that hail? No, wait. Carrie's heart stuttered. *Could it be...?*

Yes, pebbles on her windowpane. For her. Ryan had come for *her*. A little flutter beat in her chest as she rushed to her bedroom window. Peering out, she saw him atop a horse from the Moore stable and leading Cooper. Right, he didn't have horses of his own. She smiled. Couldn't help herself. Glad of the oversized T-shirt she wore as a nightdress, she eased up the sash. She leaned out, conscious of Sammie asleep down the hall, and Adam snoring from the floor beside the girl's bed, and said in a loud whisper "What are you doing?"

He grinned up at her. "Come riding with me."

Thrills raced through her body, almost bursting out of her fingertips. He sat astride Adam's horse, a dark bay mare named Eclipse. Moonlight lingered over his form, making quite the alluring picture. He used to come for Hannah to take a moonlight ride. Sometimes by horse, sometimes in his fourth-hand truck. Carrie had always wished a guy would show up for a ride with her, but her boyfriends hadn't been the Romeo type.

Nor was this that kind of scene. This was Ryan,

doing as he said at the dance: simply being. Falling into old patterns, but she didn't mind.

She'd take his advice and not think about tomorrow. It would sort itself out.

"I brought you a piece of wedding cake."

Her whole body beamed. "You did not."

He nodded. "Stole it right from the bride's mama as she wrapped up the leftovers."

"Not the cake top!" she protested in alarm.

"Shhh."

"But that's for their first anniversary."

"You'll wake the house. Come down here to scold me."

She shook her head at him, then, afraid he might misinterpret the action, she said, "Let me grab a wrap."

"I have a blanket."

Carrie paused, swallowed. Reminded herself tomorrow was tomorrow's problem.

She ignored her jitters as she changed into jeans, a tee, and proper underclothes. This was Ryan, simply being. No fuss, no pressure. Intending to have a peaceful ride.

In the moonlight. With a blanket.

She ran down the stairs as quietly as she could. How had her sister ever gotten out the door as a teenager? Of course, Dad and Mom had awakened, and both had waited until she returned before sleeping again. At the time, being kids, they hadn't known that. It had seemed a grand adventure. Sweet Hannah being wicked and getting away with it.

Was Carrie being wicked now? Grabbing a jacket from the hook by the door, she again shook away her worries. Tomorrow would take care of tomorrow. For now, she slipped a six-pack of peanut butter crackers and a bottle of white wine from behind the potholders into a knapsack and raced to the door.

She pulled up short with her hand on the knob. Turned and scribbled a note she left on the table. *Took Cooper for a ride with Ryan on Eclipse ~ C.* Just in case tomorrow came without her in her bed. One could never be too careful or too responsible on a ranch. Snatching up her camera, she eased out of the front door.

The night air fell as softly on her skin as it had at the wedding. She couldn't help her grin, relieved to see Ryan wore one equally as goofy. Simply being had its merits.

They rode out without talking, the horses and the moonlight determining the path. The breeze and the rhythm of the horse's gait eased her mind. Why didn't she do this more often?

"Cooper loves to run at night," she told Ryan. "I forget to push away the paperwork and indulge him." She patted Cooper's neck. "We both need a break sometimes, don't we, boy?"

"You do."

She cut Ryan a glance. "I wasn't talking to you."

He laughed, the sound free on the night wind. No one laughed out on the ranch these days. She hadn't realized it till now.

"What's in the backpack?" he asked.

"Snacks."

"I brought apple juice."

This time Carrie's laughter floated on the breeze.

They rode for another fifteen minutes, not really going anywhere, until she realized Ryan had steered them to a flat spot with a gorgeous daytime view of the ranch. They were halfway to the old homestead where Grace and Mike Torres now lived with his brother and sister, past a small stand of trees. No one to see them but the stars and the moon.

"Would you like to stop out here for a bit?" he asked.

She nodded. Snack time. Stargazing.

And?

Simply being, she reminded herself.

"Wait." She positioned Cooper and retrieved her camera. When she lifted it, Ryan protested, but she continued shooting. "I'll be done quicker if you sit still."

"I feel stupid."

"You don't look stupid, and with the moon behind you, no one will know it's you." She kept clicking as she talked, used to calming or distracting clients. "You're an anonymous cowboy, out with his horse under the stars."

His posture relaxed. Exactly what she wanted. "Hold still."

"Now what?" But his grumble came under his breath so she could ignore him.

Dismounting, she hid her smile. "Different perspective."

She shot a few from the lower angle with the moon behind him, making him a true silhouette. "Done. Thanks."

While he dismounted, she took the other treasures from her pack. Ryan spread the blanket while Carrie saw to the horses. Then she set the knapsack on the corner of the blanket and plopped down on her back to gaze at the sky.

"Make yourself at home," he said with a smile in his voice.

"Stop complaining. There's plenty of room for you."

He lay beside her, a good arm's length away, and tucked his hands behind his head. "Best part of the day is night. I never take advantage of it enough."

"Work."

"Work," he agreed. "Then when I'm done working, and I've got Sammie asleep, I need to be sleeping too. Bronc riders can't very well sleep on the job."

She smiled. "That rocking horse isn't peaceful enough for you?"

"The rocking is fine. It's the falling that'll wake you up."

Carrie waited a minute, watching the stars twinkle, listening to the night creatures chirp, croak, or wing their way through the sky. "Does it hurt?

When you fall?"

"Sure does. If I land right, the impact isn't worse than tripping over a rock. If I land wrong, it'll leave a bruise. And if I land really wrong, I wind up out of competition till the doc clears me."

And if he landed really, really wrong, the horse would trample him. She pushed away the thought and wiggled more comfortably on the old quilt he'd brought. "But landing a little wrong means you get to come home."

"Yeah."

She shifted to her side and propped up on a bent elbow to study him. Not that she could see much detail of his face in the dark, but she hoped to read his posture change to judge the truthfulness of his answer. The dark outline of his body appeared peaceful, and the moonlight showed his expression as he turned to her. "Did riding out here hurt you? Jostle your arm?"

"Nah. I'm mostly healed."

"Oh." She watched her finger trace a pattern on the old quilt he'd brought. She lost herself in imagining ladies working on this at the turn of the last century. Prairie lily, she half-remembered hearing it called. Had her great-grandmother been part of the sewing bee? Her finger encountered mending stitches, indicating this blanket had had many years of use. Somehow having old timey tradition represented here in this moment made her feel more grounded.

Ryan rolled to his side, propped himself up as she had. Closer. "I'm going to have the local doctor check me out soon. Once he issues his recommendation for the rodeo doc to give me the all clear, I'll have about a week's worth of work before we head out."

She looked at him, his earnest expression twisting her heart. "That's good news, I guess."

"I want to be straight with you. So you know what to expect."

"I'll miss you and Sammie."

He extended his left hand and lifted her chin until they locked gazes. "Sammie and I will miss you too."

Her breath wouldn't come. His fingers touching her face felt too much like a caress. But he meant to leave. Soon. As soon as he could.

She jerked to sitting and reached for her

backpack. "Want a cracker?"

He didn't answer and she didn't turn. The cellophane popped like gunfire as she tore it open. She felt Ryan come to a seated position beside her.

"I'll take one. Want a juice?"

Such mundane words. Maybe he didn't feel any tension brewing between them. Maybe this jiggle of awareness only existed on her part, the moonlight and a handsome cowboy taking her on a picnic. "I brought wine."

"Sounds better than juice."

She grabbed the neck of the bottle then gave a silent head shake. "No glasses."

He took the bottle from her, holding his hand over hers for an extra moment. "I don't mind sharing if you don't."

She shook her head.

"You can drink first then."

"No, I mean, I don't mind sharing. There's this old black and white movie," she said as he cracked open the screw top. "Bette Davis has this actor— can't recall his name—light her a cigarette. And they stare into each other's eyes. The music swells like the moment's got deep meaning. Like, how could they be so scandalous. What's the name of that movie?"

He paused. "And I would know that, why?"

She chuckled and handed him a cheddar cracker sandwich with a peanut butter center. "No idea."

"What made you think of it?"

She shrugged, feeling awkward. "Drinking from the same bottle, I guess."

"Ah." He held the wine toward her. "You first."

She took a few sips. She didn't really care for wine, but she kept a bottle hidden in case one of her friends visited. Fortunately, wine wasn't Adam's choice either, but she feared one of these days it wouldn't matter what kind of alcohol he found. She'd read of alcoholics rooting around their medicine cabinets for a hit of cough syrup. Adam made her keep the Scotch she preferred in the cupboard above the sink, as a constant test for himself. Torturing himself, she often accused, but she didn't throw it out. She kept track of the volume, relieved it only changed when she poured herself a drink.

"It's actually pretty good with the crackers," she noted with surprise.

He drank and then swirled the bottle, waving fumes toward his face with his other hand. "It's made from the sweetest of grapes."

"As though I'd know anything about wine. I bought it because of the swan on the label."

Ryan chuckled.

"Lexie and I normally have iced tea, and I don't usually drink beer unless we're at Kerr's dancing or listening to the band." She sighed. "Haven't done that much lately either."

"Work?"

Carrie chewed a cracker bite and swallowed, shaking her head. "She has a husband and stepchild these days. They take up her time, as they should. Once she's settled into motherhood and being a wife, we'll make a date."

"In the meantime..." Ryan held up the wine bottle.

She took the bottle and drank.

"You need to make time to do something other than work."

Carrie turned to look at him. Had he moved closer? He sat not a foot from her, leaning near. She swallowed and nodded. "I know."

She glanced around, the moon like a spill of milk across the dark land stretching before them. "I remember your first night back, explaining to Sammie about your moonlight rides with Hannah." She smiled. "Are you planning on pulling my hair or spitting on my boots?"

"Wasn't on the game plan, no."

She tipped her head down and looked through her lashes at him with a soft smile. "What was on the game plan?"

Immediately, she stiffened in shock. "Oh my god—am I flirting with you?"

Ryan chuckled. "I believe you are."

"Am I doing it right?"

"I believe you are."

They laughed. After a moment she asked, "Is this weird?"

"No, not at all. Is it weird for you?"

"No. It's surprising, but not in a bad way."

"I know. I've never thought of you like this."

She nodded. "You only ever had eyes for Hannah. And to me, you were just the kid next door, then you started dating and you became an extension of her. Ryan and Hannah, a matched set."

"I'm not disputing anything you're saying, but you're kind of killing the mood."

She winced. "Sorry."

"Should we try kissing?"

"Well, yeah. Might as well get that out of the way."

He laughed. "You're sure not easy on a guy's ego."

They drew nearer, tentatively, eyes locked. Carrie swallowed, more nervous than she wanted him to see. Would a kiss ruin their relationship as in-laws? Make things awkward when it didn't work out?

"You're thinking too much." Then his lips touched hers almost cautiously, as though testing the temperature of a chili pepper. After a few seconds he eased away and studied her. "Okay so far?"

She nodded, her stomach spinning. This felt normal, like the excitement and anticipation and attraction she'd feel for any new man. He wasn't new, and yet he was, in this way.

"You're thinking again," Ryan said.

"Maybe you should do something to distract me."

"You're better at flirting than you think you are."

He set his mouth to hers, nothing tentative this time, engulfing her senses. His hands stayed at her sides, but she didn't need caresses. She got lost in the magic of his kisses. Glad she was sitting down, she felt light-headed and powerful at the same time. Because Ryan was just as affected. Their breaths panted out, their pulses drummed against each other. Then their hands flew, stalled, pressed, caressed. She'd been wrong. She needed his hands on her, molding as though she were clay. Smoothing as though she felt skittish. But she didn't. She felt marvelous and free, like she could fly.

"It's just that with you," she said as they caught their breaths, "I worry about messing it all up. There's more at stake than a romance."

Ryan nodded. "Let me say this fast and be done with it. Part of me will always love Hannah. I hadn't thought about the future, when I planned to date again, much less get married. I just wasn't ready. But then, all of a sudden, you were there. Like *boom*." He shot his hand back, spreading his fingers. "A firework exploding on my horizon. I didn't see it coming. I didn't see you coming."

He cupped her face with his palm. "I would've

said I wasn't ready to feel anything for another woman. And, sorry to say this, but certainly not with you. It never occurred to me."

He paused. Smiled. "Until it did."

"Well." Carrie blew out a breath. "That's certainly honest."

He trailed a finger along her cheek, moving a strand of hair the breeze had loosened on the ride. Tingles of awareness tickled along her skin. His kiss, his touch, his nearness all made her feel like her blood was carbonated.

She laughed. "Kissing you makes me feel all floaty inside."

He smiled. "I'm glad."

"It's you. It's like I know you, but I don't know you, not this way. I guess I've always thought you were handsome—after you stopped being a gawky teenager..." She stopped when he grimaced then laughed.

"Gee, thanks."

"But in a way that was well-suited to match Hannah. When I looked at you tonight at the reception in your suit, I felt this new thrill. When you took the flower girl to the dance floor, all my girl parts perked up to take notice."

Ryan studied her for a long moment, long enough to make her nervous that she'd said too much. Until he spoke. "You, Carolyn Moore, are dangerously good at flirting."

She gave him a slow smile she hadn't used in forever. The next few minutes were lost in his arms, breathing him in. She couldn't get enough of Ryan. As though she'd been starving and someone let her in the kitchen, telling her to have as much as she wanted. And boy, did she want Ryan.

She gazed into his beautiful eyes. "I can't believe we just found each other. It's like magic."

"It's crazy, isn't it. I mean, it's not, and maybe that's what's craziest of all."

They lay merely gazing at each other. Thoughts crept through her mind. What if he hadn't come home to recuperate? Would they ever have discovered their attraction in this way? She knew almost everything about him, and yet, in some ways, she had so much to discover. What was he like on the circuit?

Darn it, why did she have to think about the rodeo?

"I'm going to miss you even more now."

"I'm coming back," he whispered.

She didn't want to hear talk of him going away—or anything else. She loved this state of simply being, without a real world to attend to, with all its messy complications. So, she nodded and inclined toward him the merest inch. Not so it would be noticeable if she read the situation wrong, but handily in reach if he meant to kiss her again.

Which he did.

The lightest brush of his lips against hers made her lean in farther, chasing his kiss like a moth enchanted by a lightbulb. Closer, kissing him back. They drew apart, lips clinging in protest at the tiniest separation. The noises of night creatures faded. The horses even stood silent as though asleep, or at least shirking their chaperone duty. Only Ryan existed. Only Ryan's arms around her. Only Ryan's mouth on hers.

He eased to his side, taking her with him to snuggle together on the blanket. She couldn't get enough, but his kisses stayed soft and lazy. No urgency existed under the night sky. No one but the moon to see their caressing hands as they learned the texture of skin, the shape of the other's body. She followed the swells of his muscles with her palms; he traversed her dips and curves. It was exquisite, and lovely, and now.

They separated to draw breath, to gaze at each other, her hoping the amazement didn't show on her face. This was Ryan. Kissing her. *Her.* She'd never dreamed of it before this past week. The reality won out over dreams.

For a while they lay on their backs, fingers entwined as they gazed at the stars. Carrie snuggled in, comfortable enough to sleep out here.

"We'd better go," Ryan said in a tone denying he had the slightest intention of moving any time soon.

"We'll be covered in dew." She smiled. "Fairy spit, we used to call it."

"Charming." Humor laced the word.

Another few minutes passed before he squeezed her hand then let go and pushed himself upright. She groaned. "Come on," he said. "Can't have you turning into a pumpkin."

"That's not how the story goes. My coach is a pumpkin."

"What are the horses?"

"Mice."

"That'd be damned inconvenient to try to ride back home. We'd better head out."

Sitting up made her long for ten more minutes of lying on the quilt. Duty made her gather the cellophane and wine and stuff everything in her pack.

"Thanks for the ride," she said.

"Thanks for coming."

"Did you doubt I would?" She noticed his shrug as he replaced the blanket and smoothed the saddlebag closed. "I've always wanted someone to pitch pebbles at my window. Not you," she added quickly. "My then-current crush."

"I'm glad it was me."

"I'm glad it was you."

They rode to the barn, and Ryan offered to put the horses away for the night. Carrie decided to let him handle the tack and brush downs. She wiggled her fingers in farewell, and once out of sight, floated across the yard and up the steps to her room, holding the memory in her heart.

CHAPTER EIGHT

Carrie stretched her back, easing the muscles there after a hard afternoon at the diner. The lunch patrons hadn't been more demanding than usual, but lack of sleep had made her more cranky. She hadn't had much time in bed. And half of the time she'd lain awake, a smile stretched across her face; the other half, she'd ached with guilt and indecision.

When the young patron, Brandi, came in again, ordering a large milk and using the restroom to clean up, Carrie tossed in the towel. Literally. She threw down the rag she'd been using to sanitize the cleaned tables.

"Leo," she said after barging into his kitchen domain. "I need you to do something for me."

The grizzled man raised his brows then grunted.

"Maybe."

About seventy-something—or ninety, Carrie couldn't pin down his age—Leo played his role with grumpy perfection. He'd come to Little Tree in his late twenties or early thirties, worn out from the Army, and stayed. He hadn't taken to cowboy life, or it hadn't taken to him, after a few years of stubbornly trying to be a ranch hand. After two years of waiting tables at Kerr's Bar and Grill, he'd asked the owner to lend him money to open a diner. Story was, old Mr. Kerr had stared for a full minute then laughed hard enough to almost have a heart attack. But he'd made the loan. The Diner had helped feed the town for over forty years.

She didn't know what Leo did when not working. It seemed he always was. And she planned to help him with that.

She went closer so Brandi and the two remaining patrons couldn't overhear. The two pals had moved to a clean table to play cards. Leo would go throw them out in about an hour. "There's a customer who comes in every other day. You know her: she orders whatever the special is."

"And you give her a heaping plate and lie to her

about leftovers."

Carrie bit her lip, then tipped her head to the side in acknowledgement. Not much got past Leo. "I think she needs a job."

His hairy eyebrows crashed down. "Do I have a job to give her?"

"She can have some of my hours. And of course, a meal for whatever shift she's working. I thought maybe mornings. It's hard for me to get here sometimes when I have ranch duties to tend to."

"Is it now?"

Carrie nodded. "And if my niece is in town when school starts, I'll need to spend more time with her. Maybe run her into school in the mornings."

"Is that so?"

"Yes."

"She gonna be in town?"

"Hopefully. And even if she's not, I'm thinking of doing some of your office work, which means I won't have as much time to waitress." Carrie held her breath. He might fire her on the spot for her sheer audacity. "You're behind on the paperwork. You know you are."

Leo gave the grill a swipe with the metal flipper

then turned to her, leaning against the counter with his arms crossed. "What do you know about this girl you want to hire?"

"She's got manners."

"Uh huh."

"She tries to keep clean, but she's using our bathroom to do it, so I think she might be camping. I haven't asked who's letting her stay on their property in case she doesn't have permission."

"A trespasser?"

"Not sure, but I've always shot straight with you. She might be."

"So." Leo narrowed one eye at her. "You want me to hire a stranger no one knows anything about. Who might be trespassing. Who doesn't have a place to keep clean. Who, I repeat, we don't know anything about."

Carrie squared her shoulders. She'd worked for Leo since high school. He had a soft spot a mile wide, once a person dug down to it. "Leo, she comes in here hungry. I'm afraid the only meal she eats is the one she gets here. One meal. Every other day."

The silence stretched for a second before he sighed. "What's my new employee's name?"

"Brandi. I don't know her last name."

Leo glowered at her. "You interview her. See what your gut tells you. She'll be taking some of your hours, so make sure you want to do this. You and I will talk later about whether you'll be working in the office or not."

He was bluffing. She hoped. Giving up pay wouldn't be wise.

"If she passes muster," he continued, "you can start training her. Four hours for four days. If she ain't mostly picked it up by then, she never will."

"Thank you, Leo."

"She gets starting wage plus tips."

"And a meal."

"Well, of course a meal. I don't have insurance enough to cover any of my employees fainting."

Carrie took a step forward and Leo held up a hand. "Don't even think of hugging me. You might be bringing in a murderer for all I know."

"I'll make sure to ask her."

He turned back to the grill. If the muttering under his breath included words like "interfering" or "troublemaker," Carrie chose to ignore him.

She had to think of a way to get this unknown

Brandi person to agree to the job. But first, maybe, to get her to be less unknown.

Putting on a smile, Carrie took her a milk and a water. She checked on her other patrons, the card players, then returned to Brandi. "Do you mind if I sit?"

The startled girl shook her head.

"Hi. It's Brandi, right?"

She nodded, a wary expression in her eyes.

"And I'm Carrie, if you forgot." Carrie paused, but the girl said nothing. "I wondered if you planned to stay in the area long."

Brandi's eyes grew wider, and if possible, she paled even more. She'd tensed so brittlely, being hit by a straw might break her. "I—I... Why?"

"Nothing bad." Carrie groaned. "I'm making a mess of this. What I'm trying—and failing—to ask is if you're going to be around, what would you think of a job here?"

"A job?"

"A few hours a week to start. If you haven't waitressed before, I can show you the ropes. But it's not hard to learn, and the regulars here won't give you a hard time if you mess up at first." She grinned.

"I should say they might give you a hard time, but it'll be friendly."

Brandi had yet to move, simply watched her with those big deer eyes.

"I'm going to be working more in the office," Carrie went on, deciding to drop her voice for this next bit. Leo couldn't overhear, but the two guys playing cards might, and if her next gambit got back to Leo, there would be hell to pay. "Our owner, Leo, is getting old. He can't wait tables and cook and keep up with paperwork like taxes and payroll. He honestly needs a new payroll system. So, I'm going to need someone to help me out waiting tables. I can't stand to see him so overworked."

Carrie took a breath. She kept her smile in place but doubted it came off as genuine. The girl would probably run if Carrie didn't maintain eye contact.

"I've never waited tables."

Phew. Even though it was a check against Brandi, at least she'd spoken.

"I can teach you. There are only a few entrees besides the daily special. The only time it gets busy is when we get fresh caught fish in. People come out of the woodwork for that. But I'll work those meals with you."

She smiled hard at Brandi.

"Why me?"

Carrie wished she'd thought of this question, but the idea of giving Brandi a job had hatched less than a half hour ago. Still finding its legs.

"Why not you?" *Brilliant. Let the girl talk herself out of the job.* Trying to prevent that, Carrie rushed on, "You seem nice. You're well-spoken and polite. And I don't think you already have a job, so I'm hoping that means you're available. Most of the people our age around here are either busy on their families' ranches or trying to get out of town."

"I'm interested."

Carrie almost sagged with relief but disguised it by quoting the starting rate. "You also get tips, plus a meal."

"A job would be a godsend. Thank you." She rubbed her palms on her pants, a nervous gesture she'd used before. "I guess I need to meet Leo formally now?"

"When you're ready."

Brandi's nod was so brave, Carrie wanted to cheer. "Glad to have you on the team. Can you start tomorrow for breakfast?"

"I can. And thank you."

"Leo's the one paying you. I'll let you thank him once he finishes cooking your lunch."

Carrie rose to go but stopped at the tableside. "Oh, and are you a murderer? I told Leo I'd ask."

A laugh bubbled out of Brandi. "No murders."

Carrie nodded and turned away.

"That can be pinned on me."

Carrie skidded to a halt then turned slowly.

Brandi grinned.

~~~

Carrie dreaded what she had to do.

She'd called Matt to meet her after work, which would be late for him. Ranch managers worked past moonrise and rose before the sun. Given the ranch owner he worked for had to be ninety years of age, he usually made the men coffee at the least every morning. The Olsteen's bunk cook was in his seventies, and most days could be relied on for eggs or egg pocket wraps to go. Some days, the hands had to throw together a lunch for themselves, and Matt always helped.

Carrie had other regrets than the time, however.

She couldn't go on seeing Matt when she had growing feelings for Ryan. Even if that ... relationship? romance? or whatever-it-may-be didn't develop, the other night's ... intimacies? make-out session? or whatever *that* was had shown her she didn't love Matt. Not in the forever after way. Setting him free was the only fair thing to do.

But painful for them both.

She had deep feelings for Matt. Friendship, trust, respect. She'd relied on him as her ranch manager for years. He'd been a comfortable companion and a man she enjoyed spending time with.

If Ryan hadn't come home just now, and if she hadn't been thunderstruck by him—a reaction that still mystified and delighted her, she might have developed a long-term, serious relationship with Matt. Marriage even, if they could figure out the logistics of her co-owning the Moore Ranch. Adam hadn't indicated he wanted the responsibility of being the ranch boss, and she hated to push him.

Flipping to the Closed sign as she saw the last customer out the door, Carrie braced herself for the scene to come. Brandi had offered to come in after closing to clean the bathrooms, and Carrie wondered if she wanted the privacy to wash up. She'd have to investigate that in the coming days. Thankfully, Leo had left at nine, leaving her on her own for the past hour. She'd rehearsed what she needed to say, discarding so many versions she didn't know if she had the right words now. Sanitizing the tables gave her time to think.

Until the bell rang over the door. She turned, dread in her stomach.

"Hi, Matt. Would you turn the dead bolt so no one comes in?"

She ignored the startled look he gave and brought two glasses of iced water. She pecked his cheek and indicated the booth least visible from the street.

As he drank some water, he studied her over the rim of the glass. Setting it down, he leaned his forearms on the table. "This sounds serious."

She nodded, grateful for the opening. "We can't date anymore."

Her inward groan covered any verbal response he might have given as she closed her eyes in disgust at herself. What happened to her carefully worded speech? He deserved more than a blurted-out rejection.

Matt leaned back in the booth, too cowboy to slump, but putting space between them. No easy contact possible.

Carrie couldn't think of a thing to say to make it better. She couldn't retract her words and doubted he'd hear her apologize for bursting out with them. Some things were better done fast.

Though his silence did concern her. Being a cowboy, he didn't wear his feelings on his sleeve. He didn't react any differently than if she'd said she was buying a few more head of cattle.

Actually, that might have gotten a reaction.

After another minute of silence while she tried not to fidget, Matt blew out a huge breath. "I can't say I'm not disappointed, but I also can't say I'm surprised."

Carrie froze. Were her feelings for Ryan so transparent?

"We've barely spent time together since I left your ranch for the Olsteens'."

"I'm sorry about that. That you left."

He shook his head. "I needed to. At your place,

I'd always be the second-tier manager. You're too active an owner to have ever given me the responsibility I wanted. I'm the ranch boss at Olsteens' in more than title."

"I'm glad it worked out."

"I told you at the time I had other reasons for leaving Moore Ranch than just to date you." Matt pointed at her with a wicked grin. "You didn't believe me."

She ducked her head, embarrassed at her vanity. "Guess you weren't just being gallant after all."

"I spend more time with you here at the diner than we spend on dates, and that's because I make the effort to come in."

"I'm sorry."

"Nothing but a fact. It was easier for our feelings to grow when I worked at Moore Ranch. Working side by side. Spending so much time together."

Carrie nodded. "Proximity."

"We also have a lot of interests in common. Our outlook on life, love of the land, belief in the future. We'd have made a good team."

"But I'm too busy. Managing the ranch,

wrangling the house stuff, working at the diner, and trying to keep up with my photography." She sighed gustily. "It's a lot."

"Your schedule, mine." He waved it all away. "They're excuses. We would've made time to be together if we couldn't stand to be apart."

"I hadn't thought about it like that." She'd fit him into her schedule as she could. Which sounded awful now he'd pointed it out to her. Had she seen it, it would have been a madly waving red flag. Fortunately, Matt had been aware they were drifting apart and had foreseen this conversation.

"So." He propped his elbows on the table and leaned toward her. "You're starting up with Ryan Winslow?"

Her face heated. She hadn't mentioned Ryan, so her feelings must be obvious. Or maybe Matt was a talented guesser. "I don't know. Maybe. It may not go anywhere. But the fact that I'm torn told me I was being unfair to you."

"As a friend, I have to ask. Are you sure that's a good idea, being with your sister's husband?"

She winced.

"Your deceased sister, I mean. Sorry." He

shrugged. "Not sure that sounds better or easier. Or smarter."

"I'm not sure it's any of those things. It just *is*."

He nodded. "And that's what's missing between us."

"You're making this extremely easy on me."

"I guess I'd be more upset if you were deeper in my heart."

She winced again but followed up with a smile. "Ouch."

"Even knowing this was probably coming, I didn't know how I'd feel. But the fact I didn't think up a plan to stop it from happening says something, right?"

"Right. So, we're okay? Still friends?"

Matt hesitated then nodded. "We will be."

He rose, placed a warm palm on her shoulder and showed himself to the door.

Honestly, they'd said all they had to say, and sitting together would have become awkward. Carrie slumped in the booth, wishing Leo served something more fortifying than Coca-Cola. She ran through the day's offerings and considered finding a spoon and a pint—or tub—of ice cream when the back door by the kitchen opened.

"Oh!" Brandi froze like the proverbial deer, eyes wide.

"It's only me." Carrie crossed the room in time to see Brandi toss a backpack through the men's room door.

"Cleaning supplies."

"We have our own," Carrie said calmly, sure now Brandi meant to take a sink bath. The girl had begun to worry her.

They both spun as the front door opened, bell ringing merrily. When Carrie recognized Adam coming in, she relaxed and turned to Brandi. She hadn't realized she'd stepped in front of the younger woman, probably alarming her, given Brandi's lack of color and tense posture, as though about to flee.

"It's just my brother."

"That's a nice greeting," he said as he neared them.

Carrie stepped aside. "Brandi, this is Adam, a constant pain in his sister's behind, but a decent guy if you didn't have to grow up with him. Adam, this is our new waitress, Brandi."

Adam tipped his head in a nod, Western cowboy-style. Not getting too close, not being too trusting, but not disrespectful. His gaze took in her measure, but he kept any reaction to himself. "Nice meetin' you."

"Same." Brandi breathed out the word.

Well, her brother could take a woman's breath, Carrie supposed. Tall, dark, handsome. Cowboy. The combination went to some women's heads. She might have to talk to Brandi about being charmed by the cowboys around here.

"I came to see if you were okay."

"I'm fine." She turned to Brandi with a smile, trying to make her overbearingly male brother less intimidating. "He's always protecting me. I might joke about him being a pain—and sometimes he is—but I appreciate it."

Brandi nodded but didn't appear reassured. Could be because Adam's body had taken on his Protector Stance, all tense and ready to do battle. Or maybe because this late, Brandi had expected an empty building.

"What's up?" Carrie asked him.

"I saw Reynolds leaving. He looked..."

Despite the sad circumstances under which

Matt had left, Carrie had to stifle a laugh as her brother floundered for a description. She doubted a born and bred cowboy like Matt had done anything to show his feelings. Less likely would be Adam's ability to figure out the other man's tamped down emotions. Adam's brotherly radar had detected a problem of some sort. That struck her as both lovely and unexpectedly astute.

"We broke up." When Adam's brow lowered, she added, "I broke up with him."

Adam grunted. "'Bout time."

After a glare for him, she turned to Brandi. "Do you have a brother?"

Brandi paused before shaking her head no.

"A sister?" Carrie wondered aloud.

Another head shake.

"You poor thing. But at times like these, I'd have to say, *how lucky.*"

"All right, all right," Adam said. "Enough abuse. You headed home?"

Carrie raised her brows in question at Brandi.

"I'll be fine," Brandi said. "I'm just cleaning toilets."

"Nice one, sis," Adam said. "Pass off the cra-, uh,

worse job to the new hire."

"Oh, no, I volunteered."

"She only made you *think* you volunteered."

"No, no—"

"Ignore him," Carrie cut in. "He's poking at me. Don't forget to lock the back door, okay?"

"You can trust me."

"I do. Yes." She turned to Adam. "I'm ready to go."

Hopefully there'd be a quart of rocky road in the freezer at home.

~~~

Carrie took a breath, both anxious and eager for Ryan's visit. She had rehearsed her sales pitch to him, laughing at her tendency to over-plan and then end up winging it, as she had with Matt. Encouraged by the thought of their breakup turning into an eventual friendship, she hoped today went as well.

Because this would be trickier.

A quick two-rap knock sounded on the screen door before Ryan walked in. Her heart quickened with pleasure at the sight of him. Fortunately, she had a thing for cowboys because this man lived cowboy through to his bones. She had to remind him the rodeo was only one aspect of cowboy life. He could be doing so much more. Here. Or next door. With her.

She snuck in another breath as he crossed the room and took her outstretched hands.

His lovely eyes searched her face. "I left Sammie with Adam in the barn as planned. I think they're searching for the kittens."

"She does love them." Carrie stretched up and kissed him briefly.

"Hey." He grabbed her waist and pulled her flush against him. "Where are you going?"

When his lips settled on hers, she met him with enthusiasm. These rare stolen moments with no Sammie or Adam or the town to see them had to be appreciated. By the time they drew apart, they were both breathless.

"Better," he said, and she nodded.

Keeping his hand in hers, she led him to the kitchen table, where all serious discussions took place. She retrieved the glasses of ice from the freezer and poured lemonade from the pitcher she'd set out. The papers she had to show him remained on the counter as she sat at the table across from him.

She asked about his progress at Windy Glade.

"It'll be a while," he said, and her heart sank. "I'll have to rent it out at least through this year, get some income any way I can."

Maybe, she wanted to say, you and Sammie could live here at Moore Ranch. But it was way too early in their relationship to suggest that, even them moving in platonically. Though a voice in the back of her head insisted the ranch house had ample room. She hushed it. *And what about Adam?* she argued with that bedeviling voice. This was his home, his inheritance too. He and Ryan would have a hard time living under the same roof.

"Sam and I won't need much," he continued, "while we're on the road."

Okay. The time had come.

"Do you have to return to rodeo? For sure?"

Ryan nodded. "That's my income source, for now. I can't move forward with any plans at Windy Glade without money."

"True." She rose and retrieved the papers from the counter. She held onto them at the table, despite Ryan's raised brows. "It's going to be hard to see where a relationship between us is going if you're on the circuit."

"I know." He raked a hand through his hair. "I want to explore that too, explore us, the possibilities ahead."

"I was thinking..."

He filled in the pause. "Should I be worried?"

She shook her head, not sure about the answer, and pushed the school enrollment papers to him.

He drew back sharply with an inhalation and stabbed her with his gaze. "You still want to take Sam from me?"

"No! Of course not. But Sammie needs to start school. This is merely to enroll her for the fall."

"Enrolling her at Little Tree Elementary means she's not with me, Carrie. That's not acceptable."

"But—"

"She gets education on the circuit. I told you about Callie, didn't I, the young woman who plans to be a teacher? She's good with the kids. And Sam needs to be with me."

"She needs to go to a real school."

"What do they learn in kindergarten anyway? Stuff I can probably teach her." He leaned forward. "Because. She'll be. With me."

"Ryan." Carrie took a breath to calm her nerves. "Kindergarten is more advanced than even when you and I went. And there's more to her attendance than the three Rs. She'll meet the other kids she'll go through school with for the next twelve years."

He crossed his arms over his chest. "Sounds like she has plenty of time to meet them."

"Kindergarten is about being away from your parents, having some freedom—which one might argue she has too much of on the rodeo circuit."

"She's safe. Sh—"

"I don't doubt that."

He closed his mouth, surprise on his face. "Thanks for that at least."

"I can be her temporary guardian. I should have some kind of official backup status anyway, even if you were both on the road. To make sure she's cared for in case something happens—something *worse* happens to you next time."

Ryan's face shuttered.

Okay, moving on. She'd save that fight for another day.

"She'd have stability here. Learn ranch life instead of rodeo life."

"She'll learn that once we move back."

"And how old will she be then? How far behind in school?"

He narrowed his eyes.

"Because it's going to be hard to be a ten-year-old in first grade."

Ryan rose, oh so slowly, and walked away. He stood facing the window over the sink, hands braced on the countertop.

She wanted to apologize for that last crack but decided it served its purpose. He needed to think about the effect on Sammie.

In its best version, Sammie would have supervision at all times; be kept safe from men, boys, animals, and the dubious role models of buckle bunnies. She'd receive a good educational foundation, explore her artistic talent, and have well-mannered friends her age. She would build a social foundation, discover hobbies, have three squares a day, and a safe, familiar place to lay her head. And a pet.

That wasn't much to ask, but Carrie doubted it was easy to provide on the circuit. Despite his best intentions and love for his child, Ryan couldn't ensure all that on his own.

Living at Moore Ranch, Sammie could have it all. Except her daddy.

And there was the snag.

"Separating you isn't ideal," she said quietly.

He snorted.

"But it might be what's best for Sammie."

"You really think being abandoned by her one remaining parent is the best thing for her?"

"She wouldn't be abandoned. She'd be living in one place, a permanent home, with her relatives who love her too."

"You haven't been paying attention. She has nightmares. She needs me."

"Maybe she's afraid of being left alone. On the road, going from one rodeo arena to another, she has no one except you. And every night you head out to ride a dangerous animal. The *best* outcome is to be thrown to the ground."

He blinked.

"She's seen you bruised, bloodied, and more seriously injured." Carrie nodded to his arm and softened her voice. "She may not remember Hannah's death, but she knows about it. She knows what's happened to other bronc riders. How could she not be terrified, when you're the only person in her world, and every night you could die like her mother? Who would take care of her then?" She blinked away tears. "How long would it take for Adam or I to get to wherever you're competing, where she'd be alone after your injury? If we even knew what happened to you. How long before we're notified?"

Ryan hung his head, breathing hard.

She let her arguments bubble in his head like stew simmering on the stove. Took her lemonade into the living room and waited to see which way Ryan would lean.

After a good four minutes, the kitchen door squealed open and then closed quietly on its latch.

He'd left, making his decision for the future clear.

And it didn't include her.

~~~

Carrie didn't let Ryan's negativity deter her. She took Sammie's visit to Little Tree as a wake-up call. She needed to work less at the diner and be more available at the ranch. Adam needed her help, in whatever way she could help without being an enabler. She needed to monitor him so she could hand over his duties as owner when he showed signs of being ready. Maybe having responsibility at the ranch would provide the motivation he needed to get sober and stay on the wagon.

She sure needed a change herself.

So far, she'd been seriously involved with a ranch manager, who'd had to play second fiddle to her, and then a man who had his own ranch. Her being the ranch manager and co-owner of Moore Ranch had been a hindrance in both relationships. As much as she loved Moore Ranch, she wanted to find someone to build a life with. She hadn't known that about herself when she dated Matt.

Which should have clued her in about her feelings for Matt right there.

She didn't know how things would play out in the future. Best case scenario, Ryan would stay and the three of them, and any future kids they might have, would turn Windy Glade into some kind of horse ranch for Ryan. In this dream scenario, Adam would straighten up and fly right, and his battle with the bottle would be over.

Carrie didn't totally believe in that vision, but

she held hope of landing close to it. The first step would be to concentrate on Adam and the ranch. She'd sort out the Ryan-slash-Windy Glade problem somehow. Safeguarding Moore Ranch always came first.

She arrived early for her evening shift to talk with Brandi. The younger woman had worked all morning and into the afternoon to help out Beatrice, who'd taken Johnny to an appointment at the V.A. in Billings.

"I want to talk to you about something," Carrie said upon arriving.

"Uh-oh."

"What's that mean?"

Brandi rubbed a hand over her lower back, twisting her head to ease a spot of tension in her neck. "Last time you wanted to talk to me, I wound up on my feet for five hours a day, toting dirty dishes, and trying to please cranky customers."

"Bad day?"

"Or maybe it was me. First shift alone and taking Beatrice's hours too."

"That was sweet of you. I really couldn't come in today."

"I stressed about it. Didn't sleep well in anticipation of being on my own, and for so long a shift." Brandi's lips lifted in a rueful smile. "Maybe the customers weren't the problem."

"We all have days like that."

Brandi untied her apron, her gaze going to the metal swing door to the kitchen. "I just hope Leo doesn't fire me."

"Hey." Carrie reached a hand to touch her briefly on the arm. "He's not going to go back on his word so easily. As I said, we all have hard days. I certainly have, and I'm still here."

"Do you think so?"

"Yes. Did anybody say anything about your attitude?"

"No." Brandi rubbed her neck. "Maybe it was me, being sensitive."

Carrie remembered being twenty, but she hadn't used the word *maybe* quite as often as Brandi did. The girl needed some confidence. She hoped her proposal for Brandi would help.

"Look, this might be a bad time to suggest this..." Carrie paused but Brandi didn't run away. "I'd like to concentrate more on my ranch and on getting

Leo's accounting in order. He's been lax about it this year. He does payroll, but the rest is binge work. You know, ignore it until he has to, then pay all his bills at once, do all the ordering at the same time, like that."

Brandi settled her hip against the counter. "Go on."

"Well, I'm going to be here in the office, which is time away from the ranch, but I need to be at the ranch, getting my own files in order. If I ever want to...I don't know, get married someday, I want it all ready to hand over to Adam."

Adam worked as one of the hands, not as a co-owner or manager. Brandi would hear about his problems from the townspeople eventually, but for now, Carrie guarded his privacy. It hurt her to say anything negative about her brother.

Instead she added, "I don't want the ranch to be so dependent on me being there. I'm not planning on leaving any time soon, but I want the possibility."

"Because you're feeling tied down now? I know that feeling."

Carrie nodded. "This week, yes. I'm torn though. I love the ranch. It's our legacy, mine and Adam's.

I'm just... I don't know. Restless."

Brandi studied her for a moment. "And how does this involve me?"

"I can't give you all my hours because I need those tips, but I'd like you to consider taking more of my shifts." When Brandi appeared ready to object, Carrie rushed on. "I know you've had a bad day and this is a stupid time to ask you. If I didn't believe you could handle it, I wouldn't suggest it. When I trained you, you picked it up fast. And at first, I'll make it a point to be here, working in the office in case you need help. But you won't."

"Has Leo agreed to this?"

"He will. He'll never fire Beatrice either, but she's in her seventies and she's got her hands full with Johnny. I think she really comes in to get a mental health break."

"Could she do the office work?"

Carrie shook her head. "Beatrice needs to be around other people. They don't have kids so it's only her husband and doctors for talking to."

"And quilting club."

"Right. They make Folds of Honor quilts for the post-military. But the group meets less often than they used to and she attends fewer get togethers."

"You've got an answer for everything."

Carrie shrugged. "I've thought about this a lot."

"Trying to get everybody's affairs settled. Are you sure you're not eloping or something?"

Carrie laughed, feeling hollow. "I wish. It sounds romantic."

"Being swept off to some romantic destination? Sure. Because we always picture the guy to be amazing: handsome, kind, and blindly in love with us."

"And maybe secretly from a royal family."

"Wouldn't hurt."

"I want to be able to go with him if a prince comes in for a burger."

"Well, how can I stand in the way of your dream?"

CHAPTER NINE

Ryan forced his feet to continue the path to the shed in back of the Moore barn. He'd seen Adam go out a time or two and learned he repaired things in the shed. Ryan couldn't help wondering if he kept a bottle hidden out there too. Which was not the mindset he needed right now.

"Hey," he said as he walked in to see Adam bent over a worktable, sanding something. Ryan handed him the bottle of pop he'd brought and held up his own as-yet-unopened beer. "Is it going to bother you if I drink?"

Adam shrugged.

Deep breath for patience. "I brought myself a pop too, just in case. I don't want to drink in front of you if the smell tempts you or something."

"Whatever."

"Look, I'm trying not to be a dick."

Adam's eyebrows rose. "Try harder."

Ryan set aside the beer and opened his bottle of Coke. "We all have our struggles, man."

"The great Ryan Winslow admitting a fault? I can hardly believe it."

Ryan narrowed his eyes. "Of course, mine are nothing on the level of yours."

After a moment, Adam laughed and saluted him with the Coke. "Touché."

"Did you know Carrie wants me to leave Sam here?"

Adam choked on his drink, then swiped the back of his hand over his mouth as he eyed his brother-in-law.

"That's what I thought," Ryan said.

"She told you that?"

"Yeah. Time for Sam to go to school."

"Oh. Well." Adam nodded. "I can't argue that."

"Neither do I. But she's getting schooling."

Adam's brows rose again. "You're home-schooling her?"

"No. God forbid. There's a girl on the circuit." He

caught Adam's jerk of the head from the corner of his eye. "Not like that. She's a kid. I don't know, nineteen or something. She wants to be a teacher. Her dad is a stock manager, so she's been traveling with us for years."

"She go to school?"

"She did, yeah. On and off, and her mom home-schooled her in her early years, so she's got the background. So, it's not like Sam's deprived or anything."

"Didn't say she was."

"Thanks."

"Didn't say she wasn't either."

"Jerk."

Adam took a minute before adding, "I'm on your side on this, though. Sam should be with you."

"I'm surprised you'd say that."

"Carrie doesn't need more on her plate to take care of. And I ... I wouldn't be much help to her right now. I'm for sure not a good role model for a kid."

"Didn't say you were."

Adam shot him a side glance.

"Didn't say you weren't either." Ryan took a swig, wishing for something stronger to drink himself.

"You're more a cautionary tale."

"So, you gave up trying not to be a dick?"

"Just wondering where you stood on this. Glad I don't have to fight you both."

"Carrie is formidable enough on her own."

Having enough of the sharing of feelings, Ryan wandered closer to the bench. "What are you working on?"

"Fixing a chair from the kitchen. Needed the stretcher replaced."

"That's the bottom rail there?"

"Yeah. Chair's been out here for a couple of months, and I finally got tired of seeing it. I sit out here sometimes to be on my own."

Was that a none-too-subtle hint to leave?

"I've been working on other, more urgent repairs. We have enough chairs."

Ryan had to do a mental recall that there were at least four at the kitchen table, to include himself and Sammie. Satisfied Adam hadn't meant to slight him, he nodded. "Nice work."

Adam shot him a glance. "Keeps my hands busy."

"Take the compliment. I wouldn't have been able

to tell it was a replaced part." Ryan wandered to the end of the worktable, inspecting the tools.

Without stopping his sanding of an intricate edge, Adam said, "Go ahead and look around. I'm sure you want to check if I have a bottle out here."

Ryan jerked in surprise at being so obvious. "Never crossed my mind."

Adam snorted.

"I'll take your word for it."

"You shouldn't."

"Why?"

"Drunks lie."

"Is that how you see yourself?"

"It's how everyone sees me. I'll be moving into the bunkhouse or the empty cookhouse if Sam moves to Moore Ranch."

"She won't be."

Ryan recalled the friend Adam had been when they grew up next door to each other. He hadn't been a friend to Adam since coming home, only riding him about his drinking and leaving everything on Carrie. "It's important to me, you know. How you see yourself."

Adam straightened and eyed him while he

finished his bottle of Coke. Then he nodded. "Fair enough. I don't think of myself as a drunk, but I am an alcoholic."

"On the wagon?"

"Currently, yes."

"Bumpy ride?"

"Always." Then Adam tilted his empty hand back and forth in a so-so gesture. "Some ruts are harder than others, deeper, and some days it's just a gravel road. But it's never going to be a totally smooth ride."

Ryan nodded as he digested this. He respected his brother-in-law for the courage it took to be so honest. Especially since Ryan had been such a hard-ass up until now.

~~~

Ryan walked in through the kitchen door, took Carrie by the hand, and led her to the living room. He sat on the couch with her on the next cushion. She tucked a leg under herself to face him. As much as he wanted to kiss her, he shouldn't. The time had arrived for a serious discussion. The local doc had cleared him to return to rodeo and assured him the rodeo doc would give him the go-ahead to compete. Which meant he had to make plans with Carrie. A kiss might sway her, not make her think straight.

He smirked. *Think highly of yourself, don't you?*

"What's funny?" she asked. "And what's going on?"

"Not funny." He leaned in and kissed her lightly. Hopefully this would be the first of many nights in each other's arms. "Or just making fun of myself."

"Where's Sammie?"

Ryan wanted to groan. So many details he left out, and frankly, didn't want to fill in. "I got a babysitter. That girl from town who works at Annie's."

"Why? You can always bring her here."

"Well." He cleared his throat. "If this discussion goes well, I might be late returning home."

She raised a brow. "That sounds promising, although a little presumptuous. What about if it doesn't go well?"

"I might need to be alone for a while. Lick my wounds."

Carrie swallowed hard. "Ryan, what's going on? Is it your injury?"

"No. Arm's fine. Shoulder's great. That's part of what I wanted to talk to you about."

"O-kay."

"I think we're—you and I are building something." He waited for her nod and blew out a breath when it came. "Phew. Okay. So." He cleared his throat. "I have feelings for you. I mean I've always had feelings for you. Friendship when we were younger. Affection for a neighbor, for my girlfriend's little sister. Brotherly love for my sister-in-law."

Carrie settled back against the couch, arms now crossed over the pillow she'd pulled onto her lap.

He'd bungled it. "But now it's more."

She blew out a breath. "Jeez, Ryan. Way to bury the lede."

He took her hand in his, facing her. "That's good, right? That I care for you as more than my sister-in-law, as more than my neighbor or friend?"

She beamed. "Very okay."

He waited. Maybe she thought those two words served some purpose, but they him brought minimal relief. "Care to elaborate?"

Carrie studied him for a moment as though considering her words. He tried not to sweat. Cowboys didn't fidget, even when the going got tense.

She took a breath. "I'm falling for you."

Relief swept over him like a warm shower on a cold day.

"Not as my brother-in-law," she continued. "Not as my neighbor or longtime friend. I'm more than halfway in love with you, Ryan."

He gathered her to him, hugged her close. Gave himself a minute as he struggled for words. She was so much braver than him. Now that it was safe to admit his feelings, he felt like a coward for not saying it first. He drew away and looked into her eyes.

"There's no halfway about it for me."

To hell with not kissing her. Whose stupid idea was that?

He drew her close, almost desperate in his need to kiss her. Their lips meshed, expressing love in the most basic way. He couldn't get enough, his hands roving over her. Seemed she felt the same, and he shivered under her caresses, hardened with desire. Several minutes passed while Ryan thanked the powers that be for letting him experience this feeling again. Little murmurs whispered through the air, answered or unheard, but none were wasted, even if not heard clearly or remembered later.

"So you're staying here, in Little Tree?" Carrie

asked.

Ryan slumped and drew back. Talk about a buzzkill. "No, I thought... I hoped, you'd come with me and Sammie."

Her eyes went wide. "On the circuit?"

"Well, yeah, considering that's where we're going to be. You can't babysit Adam forever."

Carrie's expression shuttered, like a wall thrown up between them. "I thought you might not go back. That you'd try to make a go of Windy Glade."

"I'd need money to do that, Carrie. Money I earn bronc riding, *winning* at bronc riding." Not being able to practice these past weeks worried him. What about his timing? Would his instincts return? He had to believe so. Had to.

"I thought you might get a job here, maybe with Mike Torres. You're both so good with untamed horses." She paused. Waited. Frowned when he didn't reply. "You said you planned to come home. To stay."

He nodded, holding onto his patience while she thwarted his plans. "When I have the money for building up the ranch into a business. I'll be bronc training, both horses and riders."

"I thought you planned to re-train rodeo horses into ranch horses." Her lips went thin. "Something a little safer. For you, but also for Sammie."

"That's one idea. And I might consider that later. I've spent the past two winters in New Mexico training bronc riders, so I can build on that reputation. Whenever I do it, I'll keep Sammie safe. Right now, my reputation is as a bronc rider, and I can build a business training young riders who want to learn. And I have the contacts right now, *while I'm on the circuit*—" Was she getting the idea? He had to be present to make contacts for the future. "To spread the word I'll be training riders and eventually retraining horses. But I met with Grace's husband, Mike, the other day. He's training the wild and abused already. Man, he's got something. It's almost mystical. You're right. The horses really respond to him."

Carrie shifted, pulled back, crossed her arms.

Oh oh.

"I'm glad for him," she said, "but let's keep on point. You expect me to drop everything and follow you? Because I'm not Hannah."

He took the words like a slap. Not well. "I know

that."

"And I have responsibilities Hannah didn't. When she left, Mom and Dad were alive, running the ranch. And when they died, she left it to me and Adam to run. But I can't just leave it on Adam's shoulders."

Ryan clamped his back teeth together to keep from agreeing too vehemently. Saying *you sure as hell can't* was not a way to woo her.

"I agree," he said instead, "and that's a concern. But maybe it's time to cut the apron strings, Carrie. You are the younger sister. Maybe—and I see you closing up against me, but I don't mean this as an attack or anything, but have you thought you're enabling him? Always making everything easy on Adam can't be helping him."

She glanced away, breathing deeply. Either very angry or trying to stay calm, and he hoped for the latter. He couldn't rush her, but of course she'd have to see this could be a turning point for Adam. To have to deal with some responsibility, man up.

After a few long minutes, Carrie nodded. Ryan felt like he could breathe again.

"No one knows this," she said, "but I took a week

away last year when I thought Adam could hold himself together well enough for me to leave. I went to a counselor and then attended several Al-Anon meetings. It's a support group for those dealing with a loved one who has an alcohol addiction."

"I've heard of it. Don't know anyone who's been."

"You might. We don't all talk about it. It's our life, but another person's addiction, so it's sometimes hard to be open."

Ryan considered. He suspected quite a few bronc and bull rider friends were hooked on pain pills and/or drank to excess. Drug testing occurred randomly, at least for the humans. Alcohol and drugs were easily available in every town with an arena. Hell, everywhere. He couldn't always tell who got drunk occasionally but wasn't an alcoholic versus who was. Or who drank on the sly with a real problem but held it together. And drugs? No idea. "Point taken," he conceded. "Did you learn about enabling?"

She scowled. "I learned about a lot of things. Being supportive without enabling is a tough one. Adding pressure is not recommended. And that's what it would be if I left the ranch."

"And Adam might fail. Lose the ranch."

The truth lay bare as though it had plopped on the cushion now between them. When had they pulled so far away from each other? They should be holding each other close, discussing their future. Unease churned in his gut.

"He might," she said quietly, looking down to where she idly picked at the pillow on her lap. A barrier. "But he might suffer along for a couple of years until you get back to rebuild Windy Glade and I can help at Moore Ranch again." She shrugged. "I can't predict the future. I do know, however, if Adam ruins Moore Ranch, it'll kill him. He'd never recover from that."

Reluctantly, Ryan had to admit he identified with the pressure. In his case, he was the only child, the one who bore the weight of the legacy of his forebearers. On the circuit, he felt successful and happy, but his every cell longed for Windy Glade. His parents wouldn't approve of him abandoning the land for so long, even to earn the money to maintain and improve the ranch. Pay the damn taxes. Fill the stables—hell, *fix* the stables so they could house some animals. Build a respectable-looking bunkhouse for those future students, with a decent kitchen, and hire a cook for daily meals and a housekeeper to come at least weekly.

Just making a list on the fly made his head reel. When it came to actually sitting down and planning it all, the finances would no doubt make him nauseous. He'd have to talk to the bronc association, maybe see if he could interest the rodeo in him building a bronc riders' school. One they'd help bankroll. Future of the sport, he'd insist. Not that he was the biggest name—

"Ahem."

He returned to the present. "Sorry," he said. "Thinking of our future."

At least she smiled. "Sounds nice."

"Meet me halfway?" He scooted toward her, an arm ready to pull her closer. Fortunately, she obliged, snuggling against him.

"We have a dilemma."

Carrie nodded.

Ryan had to brace himself for her answer, but he had to know. "Do you think you can come with me?"

"When?"

He'd hoped for a more enthusiastic reply. A solid

yes. "I got the all-clear today from the local doc. I'll have to close up Windy Glade, get it ready for renters."

She stiffened in his arms.

"Then I'll probably head out. Won't take more than a week, if that."

"That's not much time for me to prepare. You sound like you're going to be gone a long time."

His heart sank. He didn't miss the pronoun. Not *we*. You. "The championship's in December."

"Five months? What about Sammie's schooling?"

Dammit. She kept bringing it up, trying to tangle his feet in that trap. "Not everyone needs kindergarten. It's not even a state law. Montana allows home-schooling anyway, so she doesn't ever have to go to a school."

Carrie's jaw set. "She would benefit from the socialization."

Ryan tilted his head, moving it side to side to stretch the tension from his neck. He worked his jaw loose. How did he get so far from his plan—because this sure couldn't be counted as wooing her. This woman spun him in circles. He glanced at her, shaking his head at them both. She tied his heart in knots, a thing he definitely looked forward to. A cowboy loved a challenge after all.

"I plan to send her to school," he said. "I don't know about kindergarten, but definitely first grade. Hopefully at Little Tree Elementary."

"Or you could leave her with me."

Ryan shook his head. "I can't. Please don't ask that of me."

Carrie closed her eyes for a minute then locked onto his. "So, you're leaving?"

He gave a small nod, holding her gaze. "So, you're staying?"

Her short nod broke his heart. They held each other tightly, as though fighting any forces that would pull them apart.

Ryan wanted to scream into the sky, a long guttural cry of fury. This was unbelievably unfair. Everything had stacked up against them, just when he felt ready to love again, a thing he hadn't even known when he returned. Carrie had barged her way into his heart. He smiled against her hair, his grip easing. Probably the night she so ungraciously brought him cherry pie and plunked it down as though daring him to enjoy it.

He couldn't even blame Adam. During their talk in the woodshed, Ryan had found a new respect for his brother-in-law. The man tried to stay sober. He used woodworking and "fixing things" to keep his hands full and busy. He'd done a decent enough job babysitting the other night—that wonderful night Ryan had realized he'd fallen for Carrie. Sammie had been full of stories of Uncle Adam playing with her, feeding her, watching movies. All with a little star of admiration in her eyes. The guy was all right. When sober. And, Ryan caught and corrected himself, Adam sure to God tried to be.

Ryan had no one else to blame for wrecking his future with Carrie. Fate had brought him into the path of this wonderful, loving woman, and Fate planned to take him away again.

It was enough to drive a man to drink.

~~~

"Come and dance with me."

Adam smiled at the blonde as he drank some iced tea, debating. He'd been in and out of the booth all night with four of his friends at Kerr's Bar and Grill as they all determined to have a good time. He hadn't gone out in weeks. Reymundo had brought his new girlfriend for them to meet, but the rest had come stag. They each took a turn dancing with her, doing their private grilling to see if she measured up. Adam was happy Ashley didn't come off as snobby or too much of a party girl. She seemed like a good match for his friend.

When he'd returned from the dance floor the last time, he'd brought another iced tea for himself and a beer for her. It was a test, ordering the beer at the bar, daring the barkeep to say anything. Walking to the table without gulping back the beer or even sneaking a sip. Or worrying who watched him with suspicious judgment in their eyes.

Going into Buck's Bar in town didn't bother him unduly, though the malty beer smell reeked there, soaked into the walls, even when he ate lunch. The heavy drinkers frequented that place, and seeing himself becoming like them served as a pretty potent deterrent. But here, with families and people of all ages incorporating beer or harder alcohol into their daily lives, it all seemed so normal. So possible. He had to work to remember why he couldn't imbibe. He couldn't make drinking his "normal," even though it seemed everyone else had a better time when they added alcohol. His enemy.

The blonde greeted Rey's girl, and Adam decided to go for a spin on the dance floor with her. He took a last gulp of his tea as he eyed her. She seemed around his age but so, so young. She had the zest for life he had set aside as he tried to be a grown-up.

They danced to the live band, and he found himself drowning his worries in the noise. So what if Carrie had some idea of raising Sammie and turning their lives upside down; Ryan wouldn't allow it. He twirled Blondie out and back, sliding into the two-step pattern. She danced well and made him forget all his other troubles. They'd be waiting for him tomorrow. He wasn't supposed to plan too far forward, he recalled, as the girl spun again. One day of freaking problems at a time.

"Another?" she asked as the band slid into something slower.

He shook his head. "Need to catch my breath." When she gave a disappointed pout, he added, "But come catch me in a half hour if you're still here."

With a smile, she squeezed his hand and returned to her table of friends as he returned to his. Rey and Ashley and his three friends had taken to the dance floor, slow dancing, the latter group wooing hope-to-be girlfriends. Wooing for the night or forever was another matter he wouldn't concern himself with.

Adam settled in the booth to watch them, sliding toward his tea and taking a cool sip. As the liquid hit his taste buds, he realized he'd grabbed the wrong glass—and he swallowed anyway. The Long Island iced tea went down smoothly. God, it was good. So good.

Spit it out! a little voice cried.

But he didn't.

He couldn't.

With a peek over the rim to see if anyone in the room watched him, he took another gulp, and another, swearing at himself even as the liquid filled his soul. His taste buds separated out every alcohol: the sweet rum, the sharp gin, the life-giving tequila, the vodka, there just to add alcohol content. Even the Coke tasted better. The concoction was so sweetly scented, so strong, so alluring, he would have known not to drink it if he'd had one whiff. If he hadn't been parched, just grabbing it up to quench his thirst.

One more gulp, quick. Before anyone notices.

Then he heard himself, smelled his sour, panicked sweat, saw himself as others would. He let the mouthful dribble into the glass, caring little if anyone witnessed it. Goddammit!

He headed for the door, keeping his long stride from turning into a run. He swore in his head with every step, depositing the spit glass on the bar counter. He caught the eye of the barkeep to make sure someone knew it was dirty.

That was how he felt. Dirty. Stupid. Worthless.

He walked far enough from the door of Kerr's so no one would see him, into the darker street to the side, and leaned back against the filthy brick building. Day Zero. Again.

He wanted to curl up like a baby and cry. He wanted to punch whoever had taken away his iced tea glass, as well as whichever friend had ordered something so identical and so lethal to him. So tempting, with an almost erotic lure.

He wanted to go back in and quench the fire in his mouth.

Imaginary microscopic critters ran under his skin. His hands shook, and he imagined tucking in

Sammie with these hands. Providing he hadn't passed out on the floor when he was supposed to be protecting her. Damn his hide.

He stood coated with sweat, breathing deeply. He wouldn't bang his head backward onto the brick wall; he wouldn't break down in public. But *shit.* He'd been clean for—

Well, the number of days didn't matter now. More than seven months gone. "You did it once," he muttered then forced himself to say out loud, "You can do it again. One day at a time."

One effing day at a time.

He put it out into the universe, one of those stupid tricks supposed to help manifest his desires. "I can do this."

He'd move his things into the cookhouse. He couldn't be trusted not to drink again, couldn't be trusted to stop, and he didn't want Carrie or Ryan to turn to him as a babysitter.

He half-convinced himself it was sweat on his face that now stung his eyes. Squeezing them shut, he concentrated on his breathing. There were no bugs under his skin, he reminded himself. No fire to be quenched. Breathe in. *Wasn't your fault.* Well, not the first sip anyway. Breathe out. Breathe in. *You're in control of what happens next.* Breathe out.

Dear Lord, it's been three minutes since my last drink...

After a few minutes, he felt calmer. He still wanted a drink. He still wanted to cry. But he didn't want to punch anyone, so that was something. He rubbed his hands over his face and across his eyes. When he could see clearly, he texted Rey that he'd gone home and to tell the guys. He didn't suggest they do it again soon.

Pocketing his phone, he looked around. No one out here to see him. He thought of things other people had done in this dark side street and pushed himself upright to head home.

That was when he saw the slightest movement in the sedan parked halfway down the street.

Dammit. Someone had witnessed his meltdown after all. Worse, he thought he recognized the car. But parking here didn't make sense.

Without asking himself why, he approached the car. Once he saw the person inside, he rapped his knuckles on the driver's window.

Startled brown eyes widened as the girl

straightened. Adam suppressed a smile and gave her points for not shrieking.

Then he did smile, trying to look harmless. This girl wouldn't know better. "Hi," he said through the glass. "Remember me? Carrie's brother."

She nodded. What the heck was her name, the new waitress? After a moment she turned the ignition to Accessory to activate the window. It lowered about a finger pour. Shit. Three-quarters of an inch.

"Hi."

Now Adam wondered what the hell he'd come down the alley for. He didn't know more than two things about her, hardly enough for conversation. He glanced down the street toward Kerr's and back at ... the girl. Her rear seat held a box of food and a laundry bag. Then it hit him. "What are you doing parking here?"

"Uh." She swallowed, eyes huge and fixed on him like he might pull a gun on her. "I'd been heading out. But, well, I was tired and thought I better not drive far. So, I stopped here, in the dark, where I thought I could, uh, grab some shut eye."

"Is that wise?"

She gave a forced laugh that sounded nervous. Adam didn't believe a word she said. "Better than pulling over on the country road or being sleepy and driving into a ditch."

"Where are you headed?"

"But you're right," she said. "I probably shouldn't sleep here. It sounded smart before, but I've had a few minutes to sleep now, and I feel safe to drive. Thanks for waking me." She fumbled with the keys before managing to turn the car over. "Thanks again."

The window went up. A smile flashed his way, and she pulled out.

Brandi. That was her name.

Adam watched the little liar ease down the street. She was living out of her car. Chagrined, he wondered where she'd find to park safely for the night now that he'd chased her out of this spot in town.

He was batting a thousand tonight. Dammit. It was like he couldn't keep from screwing up.

You're in control of what happens next.

Adam sprinted to his truck, digging out his keys and clicking the fob when he neared. She hadn't been driving very fast. He could probably catch her.

And do what? Well, he'd figure it out on the drive. But he'd screwed up enough for one night. Drinking the loaded tea hadn't been all his fault. Letting the girl drive off was.

It didn't take three minutes for him to spot her taillights. He pulled behind her, knowing there was no way not to scare her. A man in a pickup truck following a woman on a deserted country road in the dark. She'd be stupid *not* to be scared, and Adam cursed himself, but it couldn't be helped. He pulled alongside her and kept pace for a few minutes. She wouldn't glance over. She tried going faster, then slower. Dammit, if they didn't wreck, she'd have a heart attack soon from sheer fright.

He put his window down and yelled her name. Did it a second time, louder.

She darted a glance his way, swerving a tiny bit. He smiled and waved.

She faced forward and kept driving.

He laughed. Well, at least she wasn't as stupid as some of the girls in those slasher movies. He eased off the gas, letting her go. When she got far enough away not to be startled, he gave a two-honk toot of farewell on the horn.

Surprisingly, she slowed. Her brake lights came on. Adam came to a full stop and waited. *Ball's in your court, Brandi.*

She executed a three-point turn and crept toward him. They sat driver door to driver door, like cops. "What do you want?" she yelled, window barely cracked, car running.

No doubt with her foot hovering over the gas pedal.

Adam fumbled. Now that she asked, what had his intention been? He rolled his window down farther. Leaned out on an elbow and smiled. Just a harmless country neighbor. "I wanted to apologize for scaring you off. If you want to go back to town and park, you should."

He couldn't make out her expression in the lights from her dashboard, but she didn't seem to be jumping for joy. "Okay," she yelled. "Have a nice night."

"Wait!"

She didn't drive off, so he counted that as a point in his favor.

He turned off his truck and slid out the

passenger side of the car. Rounding his truck bed where she could see him approach, he held his hands up as though under arrest. He stopped at the tail end of his truck, not in the road impeding her in any way. "I'm Carrie's brother, Adam."

"Good for you."

He chuckled. "If you want to follow me to Moore Ranch, you can sleep at Carrie's house tonight. I'll sleep in the bunkhouse," he added quickly. "So it'll just be you two women. And I won't tell her you're sleeping in your car."

"I was a little tired. Put my head back for—"

He shook his head and her words died away.

"I'm not stupid enough to follow you out on some..."

This time her words trailed away without him saying anything. Because here they were now, out alone on a dark country road.

"Carrie would have my hide if something happened to you. If I didn't at least try to help. I wasn't raised that way." He waited, then added, "Why you're living out of your car is your business, and I won't ask. But we don't just let that happen in Little Tree."

Her window went down an inch. He could clearly hear her say *hospitality*, though he had no idea why. There may have been another word, perhaps not so nice, muttered in front of it.

"So, you'll follow me?" When she didn't reply, thinking it over he hoped, Adam added, "Call Carrie and tell her you're coming. Or I'll call her with the speaker on so you can hear. Know it's legit."

"And that you're harmless?"

He heard the skepticism in her tone and shrugged. He'd hurt too many people in his life to reassure her. But he had never hurt a woman in the way Brandi feared now.

"We can call Carrie so you feel easier about it, or we let her sleep and I can take you to the house quietly. I'll point the way to the guest room, then go sleep in the bunkhouse. You can talk to her in the morning or try to leave before she gets up, which is, I'll warn you, pretty early. Your choice."

A full two minutes passed. Adam's patience had rubbed thin by the time she responded.

"I don't want to answer a lot of questions. Is there somewhere on your property I can park overnight?"

Her decision stunned him. Who wouldn't prefer to sleep in a soft bed, around the safety of another woman? "Carrie will kill me."

"Carrie," she said succinctly, "doesn't have to know."

~~~

Ryan walked into the Moore kitchen, closing the door quietly at the sound of little girl voices. Plural. Carrie had mentioned having a friend over for Sammie to play with, and if they were having fun, he'd duck out. As long as his daughter was fine, he had work to do.

Music played, not that he recognized it, but the giggles froze him in his tracks. How long since he'd heard Sammie laugh? He stood in the kitchen and leaned against the wall. How long? She hadn't had a nightmare since the wedding he'd gone to. He smiled, thinking of the wedding night, when he'd danced with Carrie and later gone for that ride. The night he'd seen her across the dance floor and knew why it bothered him she dated Reynolds. Knew why it bothered him that she worked so hard and took care of everyone else so lovingly. Knew he wanted to take care of her, to have her near.

But the stubborn woman was tied to the Moore

Ranch. She had the misguided belief she could help Adam, when all the literature he'd read recently said an alcoholic had to heal himself, with the help of God and maybe a sponsor with the same addiction. That family could love but not cure. Yet she intended to stay behind. To sacrifice their happiness together.

And, grudgingly, he could see her point. Moore Ranch needed someone to run it properly.

"That's right," Carrie called with a laugh. "You've got it."

Peeking around the opening, he spotted her across the room, teacup in hand, seated beside Lexi Marshall. Walker now. Lexi Walker. Which meant the other girl must be Jack's daughter. He couldn't remember her name but knew she was a few years older than Sammie. The two danced and shook and wiggled and giggled. Their movements matched the dancers on the TV, and reminded him of playing with a Hula Hoop, but without the hoop.

"Woo, Anna," Lexi exclaimed. "You got it, girl."

A tea party-slash-dance party? He grinned, reveling in Sammie's happiness, her joy of being a kid. A girl. Books sat around the room, along with a few stuffed animals. And, of course, Charming the horse.

"Oh!" she cried out, and his attention shot to her as she tripped. He took an instinctive step forward, but Carrie had already dropped by her side. Anna had sat down beside her too and took Sammie's hand.

"I got dizzy." Sam had a smile on her face, even as she put her other hand to her forehead, so he relaxed.

"Too much sugar," Lexi put in.

Carrie shook her head. "Maybe. Does it hurt anywhere?"

"No. Not...exactly."

Even Ryan knew what that meant. Sam wasn't ready to give up her role of invalid or the attention it brought.

Carrie's expression turned serious then she looked at Anna. "Do you think she needs a bandage?"

"She said it didn't hurt," Anna said, showing the wisdom and practicality of her added years.

"We should probably apply something to her wrist anyway," Carrie said. "We have some bandages with princesses on them. Unless you think we need to borrow your dad's sling?"

Sammie laughed then sobered quickly, slipping back into her role. "Just some princesses please."

Carrie hugged her. She winked at Anna. "How about you? Any place we can stick you with a princess?"

Anna shook her head. "But maybe we can play dress up in your closet."

This time Carrie laughed, along with Lexi. "We can try, but there's woefully little finery or makeup to be had in this house."

"We'll have to fix that," Lexi said, consulting with Anna. "How about we make a date next week to go shopping? Maybe have lunch at a real tea house."

"Sounds like a plan."

Ryan slipped backward into the kitchen and out the door before they caught sight of him. As he walked to his truck, his legs dragged like lead weights. Teacups, dance parties, giggly little girl friends. Princess Band-Aids, for God's sake. Dress up and shopping trips. His daughter didn't get to experience any of that on the circuit.

Kindergarten he could dismiss, or at the least, substitute with home-learning. Callie, the girl on the circuit who taught class and babysat, did a good job with the kids, and whatever Sammie needed to learn at five years old, Callie could teach her.

Except for the friendship stuff. The dancing and playing. Nor could she provide constant care. He would have jumped in to make sure his girl hadn't hurt herself in a fall, but would he have suggested Band-Aids of any sort for a wound that didn't exist? Doubtful. If he thought of it, he could serve lemonade in teacups and flip on the radio occasionally, show Sammie some old school dance moves that would make her laugh.

But he couldn't be a mother.

~~~

Ryan closed his eyes, his chest heavy and gut sick. He knew the best thing for his girl. He knew that he'd *do* what was best for her. It would tear out his soul to leave her behind, even "just" for a few months.

He sat down with her later that night in her room at Windy Glade. Spartan. Sad. "Okay, sport, I'm going to talk to you like a big girl because I need you to be a big girl now."

Sammie nodded solemnly, preparing herself, already too old for her years. She wore Carrie's pink

Walk for the Cure T-shirt. Her freshly washed hair was still drying at the scalp, and the whole damn house smelled like Carrie's soap, the Country Blush made by a local. He'd lost so much of Sammie to Carrie already, it made him ache.

But no, he reminded himself. That was good. Girly stuff. Carrie's specialty, surprisingly. Though the woman who'd stolen his heart was intoxicating and sexy, so maybe he shouldn't be surprised. She'd be a great role model for his little girl.

Ryan cleared his throat and sat facing Sammie on the bed. He took her hands in his. "Here's the thing. We need money to fix up Windy Glade. I need to ride—no, I need to *win*, and win big, in order for that to happen. For us to have a home together."

He peered at her and she nodded.

"Because that's what I'm working toward, sport. Us, together, here at Windy Glade."

He waited for another nod. Took another breath.

"Therefore, I'm going back on the rodeo circuit tomorrow, and I'm going to leave you here with Aunt Carrie and Uncle Adam."

Sammie's eyes grew wide and her mouth dropped open. She didn't make a sound, which tore at his heart almost more than if she'd let out a wail. Ryan put his arms around her and hauled her onto his lap, placing his cheek against her head and talking into her hair. Coward that he was, he couldn't face her devastation.

"I have to practice, get my timing back. There won't be much time for anything else. I'll be gone most of the day and we'd never see each other."

She pressed her face into his shirt. He felt her tears, wet and hot.

"I wouldn't be around to be sure you stayed safe, Sam. I need to know you're safe."

"I want to go with you." Her words were so hollow he could barely hear her. But he felt them into his bones.

He hugged her. "I know. I want you with me. We're a team. Always. But I have to win, Sammie. I have to finish the season. Frankly, we need the money, and this year is my best chance of finishing in the big money. Next year I'd be starting from scratch."

She didn't reply and they sat silently. Her body shook with silent tears.

Ryan squeezed his eyes shut, unable to hold

back tears of his own. Maybe Sam should see him cry. To know this wasn't easy, that it hurt him just as badly as she hurt. She didn't know it yet, but she had the better of the deal, staying here with Carrie. Going to school. Being on the ranch.

"I bought a used laptop so we can video call." The computer had been a teen's who was upgrading; Ryan was relieved to have it. "I'll probably call every day, so often you're tired of seeing my face."

He'd wait to outline all the benefits of her staying in Little Tree. If he mentioned them now, she might turn her unhappy eyes Carrie's way, and blame her, hate school, hate ranch life. All the things she might think had made it easy for her daddy to leave her behind.

"This is killing me, sport," he whispered. "I don't want to go. But it's the smart thing to do. You'll be safe and I can concentrate on winning."

She cried until she had no tears, her hiccups painful. Ryan carried her down to the kitchen, shoulder pain be damned, and held her while she drank some water. Then he carried her back to her bed. She wouldn't let go of him, so he lay down beside her, petting her hair, whispering his love.

Letting his tears drop onto the pillow above her.

When her grasp on him finally loosened as she fell asleep, she still hadn't spoken another word.

CHAPTER TEN

For the next few days, Carrie tried everything to cheer up Sammie. They watched movies. They played games. She turned on the dance party video her niece had so enjoyed the week before, but Sammie showed no interest.

Night-time stories and songs didn't have any effect. Sammie slept like a log, and despite Carrie's fears, didn't have nightmares. Even drawing or coloring didn't interest her for more than a few minutes.

She was a walking shell.

Adam had moved his clothes to the cookhouse, and, fortunately—if any part of this situation could be viewed as good—he'd moved out before Sammie moved in, so the girl didn't link the two events. Carrie did, and the guilt slammed into her every time he left the ranch house after a "visit."

Had her selfish desire to have Sammie with them run Adam out of his own home?

She'd used Grace's sister-in-law, Anita Torres, twice for babysitting, which was vital for days Carrie had to be out on the ranch with the hands. Too dangerous for Sam until she had more hours in the saddle and more confidence. On Carrie's shorter day spent in the office, Sammie came with her. She could mope as well at the diner as she could at the ranch.

Her cell phone rang, and she and Sammie both jerked toward it before freezing. It was too early in the day for Ryan to be calling, yet they both hoped it would be him. They lived for his calls. Over the past week, he'd texted her to check if she and Sammie were busy, and then she set up the video call. Seeing his face and hearing his voice had been both painful and a blessing.

Carrie shot a half-smile toward her niece, who watched with hopeful eyes, even while her body had braced for disappointment. "It's a little early to be your dad calling."

She retrieved her phone, read the Caller ID and shook her head at Sammie. Rising from the floor where she'd tried to interest Sammie in checkers, Carrie took the call in the kitchen.

After a minute, she returned and slid down next to Sammie with a smile pasted on her face. "Good news," she said perkily. "I sold a picture to a magazine. It's not a lot of money but it's a pretty big deal for me. We should celebrate."

Sammie gave a nod-slash-shrug, obviously humoring her aunt. Carrie didn't blame her. The girl couldn't understand what it meant.

"Ice cream? Or maybe dinner out?"

Another shrug.

Carrie couldn't work up much enthusiasm either. What was wrong with her? Selling this picture to a prominent Western magazine—and being asked to submit more—should have brought whoops and cheers and dancing around. Flailing gleefully like Kermit the Frog.

But having a dream come true was overshadowed by what was missing, like the moon eclipsing the sun.

A quick text as to Adam's whereabouts got an answer of him being on the far field with the hands. She'd known that, vaguely, the way she knew things these past few days since Ryan had left. Would Adam's answer have been different if she'd mentioned the sale?

Lexi's congratulations contained four exclamation points and balloons, but she'd been elbow deep in a cow—which is where Carrie stopped reading. The cow's owner had been on hand to text for her, thankfully.

"Okay, little buddy, seems like it's you and me. Let's go to Lee's Freezes for ice cream. Then once we're full, we'll drive over to the next town where they have a Micky D's and get a Happy Meal."

They could use some happy, however it came.

But neither the treat nor the drive changed their moods for more than a few hours. As they drove back into town, Carrie made an abrupt decision and swerved around a corner to the diner. Sammie's hands flew up with a surprised cry, but she laughed when she saw her aunt still in control of the vehicle.

Carrie parked and turned in the seat, facing Sammie. "Look, you're miserable, I'm miserable. What do you say we change that?"

Sammie nodded with more animation than Carrie had seen in days. "How?"

Carrie blew out a breath. "What do you say we run away to the rodeo?"

~~~

It took some time but turned out far easier than Carrie expected. She simply didn't let anything anyone said, no matter how sensible, stop her.

She started with Leo, grasping Sammie's hand as they marched past a startled Brandi and into the kitchen.

"I'm quitting."

He stilled, spatula extended over something on the grill, then turned to her in slow motion. His squint took in her determined stance, down, up, back to her face. "When?"

"Now. Sammie and I are going to the rodeo. I don't know when I'll return to town, and I don't expect you to hold my job."

"Okay."

His nonchalance left her flat-footed. She'd expected to do a lot of explaining and cajoling and convincing him she was doing the right thing. His acceptance was a little insulting. She'd worked for him for over a decade.

"You did the office work fine until I insisted I take over."

"I know."

She pursed her lips. "And Beatrice and Brandi— huh, I hadn't noticed that before, probably because I work with them one at a time. Anyway, they can use the extra hours. And if not, they can train someone. Maybe Anita Torres or her brother Paul. Shouldn't be a problem finding a teenager who wants a job. Keeping them might be more of a challenge, unless you're nice to the new hiree."

"That all?"

This man had been a true friend to her and her boss for eleven years. She needed more than a two-syllable goodbye. A laugh bubbled in her throat. *Goodbye* was two syllables. She swallowed as tears stung her eyes. "I'll miss you."

Leo set down the spatula and turned to her, arms open. She dropped Sammie's hand and dove into his embrace. He smelled like greasy hamburgers and love.

"You can do this," he said into her hair.

She chuckled and squeezed harder. "You don't even know what I'm doing."

"No. But you do." He eased her away, hands on her upper arms. "Let me know where to send your paycheck."

She sniffed and nodded. Retrieving Sammie's hand, she left the kitchen. Next on the list: Brandi.

Fortunately, only three tables held people, and they seemed to be finishing their food. She led Brandi to a booth, scooting in after Sammie. "Brandi, I'm leaving the diner."

The girl gasped, gaze flying to the kitchen door.

"Leo's cool with it. As is his way. So, the opportunity is here for you to pick up a few more hours. You can split mine with Beatrice, although I don't know how much more she'll be able to handle, both being on her feet and with her other responsibilities, though she'll appreciate any extra pay. Or you can help her and Leo hire and train someone new."

"This is so fast. Are you sure?"

Carrie smiled at Sammie, who beamed at her. "Positive."

"Well, I have to say, as much as I'll miss you, the extra money will come in handy for me too." Brandi pushed her light brown hair behind her ear. She straightened and took a deep inhale. "I guess you already know I've been living out of my car."

Carrie's mouth dropped in surprise. "What!"

"Oh." Brandi drew back. "I thought Adam would have told you by now."

"What! Adam knows?"

"Hoo boy. I'm really stepping in it today."

"Good grief. How did I not see it?" Carrie reached for her hand on the table. "What's going on, Brandi? Is there something I can do to help?"

"Quit this job and give me all your hours?" She gave a weak smile. "Oh, wait. You just did."

Carrie laughed. "Beatrice is no spring chicken, and like I said, she has Johnny to take care of, so you'll get the lion's share of the hours. But...and I don't want to be nosey, but is there anything you want to tell me? Any way I can help?"

"Maybe you should know. I have to tell someone." Brandi drew in another breath, exhaled. "I'm pregnant."

For a stunned moment, Carrie simply stared. Then she pulled herself together. "And are you okay with that?"

"I am now."

"Okay then." Carrie rose and hugged her. "Congratulations."

After much cheering and happy crying and sad crying, they brought Leo in on the discussion. Brandi would help Beatrice train another waitress. They would split Carrie's hours, with the majority going to Brandi at first, before her pregnancy affected her time on her feet or ability to carry heavy dishes.

"She ain't my first pregnant waitress," Leo grumbled.

"She'll need to eat more meals here, Leo. More nutritious."

He nodded. "She ain't my first, missy. You run along and do whatever fool thing you're about to do. The girl and I will be fine."

He rose and ambled to the kitchen.

"I see why you adore him," Brandi said.

Carrie nodded, clearing her throat. "Now, about you living in your car."

"I know, I know. To be honest, some nights I've slept in here, in a booth."

Carrie blew out an exasperated breath. "For the love of God! Are you crazy? Why didn't you tell me? I have a bedroom sitting empty at my house you could have had."

"I should have. I guess I wasn't ready to tell anyone. At least parking at the ranch felt more secure than in town. I was so thankful to Adam for letting me. Though the gas is—"

"Letting you what?" Carrie replayed and processed her words. "You've been parking at what ranch?" When Brandi didn't answer, she said, "Mine?"

A nod.

"Oh. My. God." Carrie rose, just had to walk off the information, and returned with milks for Brandi and Sammie, and a Coke for herself. She set a piece of cherry pie in front of Sammie.

"I'd like pie," Brandi said in a small voice.

Carrie narrowed her eyes. "Only good girls get pie. Not ones who keep important information from their friends."

"Is this part of the good news party, Aunt Carrie?"

She softened and patted the girl's arm. "Yes." Turning back to Brandi, she explained, "I sold a picture to a magazine."

Brandi   perked   up.   "That's   great.

Congratulations. What was the picture?"

Oh, crap. Another person she'd have to face. "A friend, Matt Reynolds. Great shot of him on horseback, if I do say so myself."

"The 'cranky customer' who helped you trick me into eating a free breakfast?"

"How did—"

"I've seen you together since then."

Carrie ducked her head. "Sorry."

Brandi squeezed her hand then drew away. "Don't be. I'm grateful. Now, anyway. I mean, I felt mortified when I figured it out, but that only lasted a few minutes. No one treated me differently, least of all you."

"Of course not." Carrie let a smile grow and grow across her face and waited until her new friend became a little worried. "But I've just thought of a way you can repay me."

When they got it all settled, which took another good half hour, Brandi was set to move into the Moore's cookhouse. She'd make breakfasts a few times a week for the hands at the bunkhouse, filling a position that had stood empty far too long. Breakfast casseroles would do for the mornings

Brandi had the early shift at The Diner. She'd make out the grocery list for the hands to pick up weekly and keep the main house presentable. Relief filled Carrie as the plan came together. Adam would have to move back into the main house now, where he should always have stayed. The world tilted back upright on its axis.

"When the work gets to be too much for your condition," Carrie said, "you can renegotiate your own terms with Leo."

"What about Adam?" Brandi asked.

Carrie glowered. "He lied to me. At least, he didn't tell me you were parking at the ranch *or* living out of your car. I am so mad about that."

"Sorry."

"You not telling me I'll get over."

"Don't be mad at Adam. Please. If he'd told you, I wouldn't have kept parking on the ranch."

"Damn straight you wouldn't, because you'd have been living *inside* the house." Carrie blew out a breath. "I'll deal with him later."

That promised to be an interesting conversation.

"I'm going to level with you, Brandi. I'd prefer if you moved into the main house, and I want Adam to stay in the house where he can protect you. I don't expect any trouble, but from out in the cookhouse, he wouldn't hear you scream. Or," she added quickly as Brandi's brown eyes went wide, "um, call for help if you were hurt or when the baby comes."

"It's his house. I don't want him to move out because of me."

He'd move back in because of her, but that was too complicated to explain.

"Now, you should know" —a pause for courage— "Adam is an alcoholic. He would never hurt you or I wouldn't suggest you move in. I'm not blind to his faults or his character, so you can trust me on this."

"I...see."

Carrie studied her, watching emotions and decisions flit across her face. She didn't know the girl well enough to figure out what they meant.

"Okay. And I guess I should tell you. I'm hiding from my ex-boyfriend."

Well now. Just when she thought the day couldn't get more surprising.

~~~

Ryan stood away from the chute, eyeing the bronc his nearest competitor was due to ride. Seven people would compete before him. He should be feeling the adrenaline, tingling with the anticipation of testing his mettle against a bronc. Not taming it, just besting it. At least for eight seconds.

Toes out, legs up, spurs in, hand flung out. He'd worked on his timing all week. He couldn't say his shoulder had healed one hundred percent, but he'd passed the frowning doc's exam.

He simply couldn't give a damn.

He hated rodeo. Hated the noise, the smells, the stock, the people. His friends had started taking the long way around to avoid him. His attitude sucked.

He didn't care.

He used to *be* rodeo. Back when it was him and Hannah and Sam.

Now he wanted to be home. He wanted to hold Sammie close to him and never let go. He wanted Carrie in his other arm, smiling at him.

To hell with this. As the rider six ahead of him mounted, he dragged the cell phone out of his buttoned-down pocket. This expense he'd cut from his budget had become his lifeline, his link to Carrie and Sammie. He kept it on him for luck, the way he'd always carried the gold dollar coin Hannah had given him for luck. He'd left that behind with Sammie, so she could hold on to a piece of him, and as a promise of his return.

The house phone at Moore Ranch rang four times before he disconnected and tried Carrie's cell. If she were out on the land, the call might not go through, but he punched her Contact anyway.

"Winslow!"

Ryan glanced at Stan, the rodeo clown, who waved. He turned his back, listening to the ringing phone. If he missed his ride, so be it.

"Winslow!"

Ryan hunched his shoulders, concentrating. Her answering message played. He stuck a finger in his other ear as Stan's voice sounded closer and louder. "Carrie, this is Ryan. I'm coming back. I'm coming home."

Someone poked his arm and he shook the person away.

"I'm coming home to you. Babe, I have to ride in a second. To try one more time for some winnings. But I don't care how well or—"

The poking finger jabbed him again.

"Jesus." He swung toward Stan with a glower. "Lay off, would you, man. I'm trying to make a call."

"There are some fans—"

"Do I look like I care about meeting any fans?" Ryan snarled before he turned away. "Sorry about that. I'll call again later. I love you. I want us to be a family. I'll see if Mike Torres needs a hand, or hell, I'll work at the garage."

Poke.

Ryan growled. "I've got to go, babe. But no matter what happens in the next eight seconds, I'm coming home."

He hit End and wheeled around. "Jesus, Stan, there used to be such a thing as privacy."

Stan, the bullfighting clown, wasn't intimidated by his glower. "These fans were pretty insistent. Want to talk to you before you ride."

"I've got half a minute."

Stan grunted and led the way. Ten steps into the walk, Ryan spotted the pushy fans. And froze.

Then ran.

Ignoring Stan's bellowing laugh, he sped to where Carrie held Sammie, both grinning like loons and waving. They stood in the walkway in the front of the rows of metal bleachers, in everybody's way. People pushing past them blurred in Ryan's eyes. He swiped at his face, not caring about the tears.

He climbed over the fence and grabbed them into his arms as his feet hit the pavement. Nothing wrong with his timing here. He pressed kisses against their heads, onto their cheeks, laughing with them. Sammie had a stranglehold on his neck, and Carrie squeezed his waist hard enough he might lose his lunch. Nothing had ever felt better in his life.

"What are you doing here?" he asked between kisses.

"You're here," Carrie said, laughing. "People who love each other should be together."

"And we love you," Sammie shouted.

He clasped them closer. "I love you too. Both of you." He gazed into Carrie's eyes. "What about the ranch? Adam?"

She nodded. "It was hard, but, Ryan, wherever you are is home to me."

He closed his eyes, his lips against her temple. "I love you."

"I'll take care of Sammie, and I can homeschool

her, even without a solid home under us. I don't care."

"Carrie, it's too much to ask you to give up."

"You asked before," she reminded him. "I was just a little slow about saying yes. Now I've got an 'in' at Western Cowboy Life Magazine, freelancing. And I'll probably get some amazing shots of you and your friends."

"I shouldn't have asked. I was selfish."

She shrugged. "Yeah, you were. And I was selfish to leave Moore Ranch. We'll deal with whatever happens later. Together."

"Winslow!"

Ryan groaned but turned toward Stan with his arms full of the girls he loved. "What now?"

"You're third up."

"Thanks."

Stan lifted a hand and walked away.

"I've got one more ride, then we'll talk."

"You've got lots of rides because you're staying on the circuit," his beautiful stubborn wife-to-be said.

"Here, Daddy." Sammie held out her open palm, the gold dollar exposed. "For your lucky ride."

He put it in his pocket and kissed her cheek. "Thanks, sport. Now I've got all the luck I could ever need."

He caught Carrie's gaze, held it. "Because I've already won."

The End

If you enjoyed this book, please help others find it by leaving a review at your favorite bookseller's site. It helps me as an author too. Thank you!

Dear Reader:

Carrie and Ryan's story got stalled by the pandemic. Many writers like me found it hard to create during the first year, which for me and many others, ran into the second year. So, this one was a bit of a struggle. By the end, I loved this book and hope you enjoyed it too.

My friends know anything is fair game, but this book has a few jokes on me. Yes, I really did buy a bottle of wine because of the swan on the label. I haven't lost this tendency, which is probably why my friends bring their own wine to parties.

If you enjoy reading my books, I'd appreciate a review posted at your favorite retailer or book review site. I'm not looking for a book report like in school. Just a few sentences will do—but no spoilers. Thank you!

You can find my Reader's Group on my website if you'd like to keep up with my releases. I promise not to bombard your inbox.

Thanks so much for reading. I appreciate my readers! You not only support my chocolate habit (wait, did I say that out loud?), but you bring joy to my writing life.

Happy reading!
Megan

Other Books by Megan Kelly

Love in Little Tree series

The Wedding Rescue
Runaway Bride
Baby Makes Three
Coming Home
Ghost of a Chance (a novella)

Marrying the Boss

Howard MO series

The Fake Fiancée
The Marriage Solution
Stand-In Mom

Christmas in Stilton series

Santa Dear
Holly & Ivey

Please visit Megan's website:
https://megankellybooks.com

To keep up to date on releases and news, sign
up for her Readers' Group on the website or follow
her Author Page on Facebook or BookBub.

Subscribe to Megan's newsletter for a
free short story, *A Risky Proposal*,
which falls before
book four, *Coming Home*.

Ghost of a Chance is a fun novella coming after
Coming Home and available now.

Authors live off reviews and if you liked this book,
I'd **love** your honest opinion. Just post it to the
bookseller of your choice or a book site like
GoodReads or BookBub. Thank you!